Incident at Five Hundred Acre Wood

From the Casebook of Lyons & Hound

Caractacus Plume

SILVATICI

For more information about the adventures of
the paranormal investigation agency of
Lyons & Hound
(est. 1895)
and to join the Caractacus Plume mailing list
visit

www.caractacusplume.com

Silvatici Publishing
silvatici@outlook.com

For
Henry Pootle
my dear old childhood friend.

With thanks to

Dr H

Louise

Mouse

Percy

Incident at Five Hundred Acre Wood

ONE
Dr Christopher Robinson

One Punch Cottage
Black Lion Lane, Brighton, England
1922

Professor Cornelius 'Dandy' Lyons gently led the smartly-dressed young man up the stairs and through to The Study, where he softly ushered him towards a leather armchair of truly extraordinary dimensions.

'Are you sure you're going to be all right, son?' he asked, with kindly concern.

'Yes. Yes, I'll be fine. Thank you,' replied the young man, his head tilted backwards and his hand pressed gingerly against one eye. 'Just a little bit shaken, that's all. No real harm done – I hope. Though it does sting like the Devil's stubbed toenail, I must say. If it hadn't been for the good fortune of your housekeeper being on the scene, I fear that I might never have found your office. I'd been searching for One Punch Cottage for quite some time, and had almost given up all hope of finding it, when some rapscallion must have thrown something decidedly sharp and pointy at me. A pebble, perhaps.'

'A pebble, you say?' sniffed Cornelius, with a twitch of his magnificent whiskers. 'My, my! Whatever is the world coming to?' he grumbled.

The dapper new arrival made to seat himself in the enormous armchair, then noticed a large red silk dressing-gown strewn carelessly across it and hesitated.

'Oo ... My apologies,' offered Cornelius, quickly plucking said garment from said chair and hastily hurling it to one

9

side. 'Weren't expecting no visitors today. Just moved in, as you can no doubt see by all the mess,' he grinned, sweeping a shovel-sized hand towards several higgledy-piggledy piles of stacked and unpacked crates and boxes that lay scattered around the room. 'Please, 'ave a seat.'

The smartly-dressed young fellow eased himself into the chair and tentatively pulled his palm away from his reddened and still weeping peeper.

''Ow about a nice cup of tea, son?' asked Cornelius, settling himself into the (less enormous) armchair opposite.

'That would be marvellous,' smiled the politely-spoken young chap. 'A great kindness. Thank you.'

As if by magic, the housekeeper, Missus Dobbs (the sweetest-looking little old lady imaginable), appeared by The Study door.

'Tea's all round, Missus Dobbs, if you'd be so kind.'

A gurn of confused terror fleetingly flashed across the face of Missus Dobbs.

'*Tea*, Ducky?' she croaked, her googly green eyes widening with alarm, before she hurriedly turned and scuttled from the room with a whispered mutter of '*Tea*? Tea! *Tea*? Oh my!'

'You'll 'ave to excuse 'er,' sighed Cornelius, apologetically, 'Missus Dobbs is new to 'er duties. Only started 'ere yesterday, in fact. But she comes 'ighly recommended.'

'I'm sure that she'll be nothing but an asset to the esteemed firm of Lyons and Hound,' offered the smart young man absentmindedly, as he wiped his twitching orb with the fold of a pristine white handkerchief. 'I'm sorry, but are you Mr Lyons or Mr Hound?'

Cornelius chuckled and twirled the drooping corners of his impressive moustache (known, by those in the know about such things, as a *Newgate Knocker*). 'Professor Lyons,' he smiled, 'at your service, sir. An' you are?'

'Oh dear. Please do excuse me. How very rude of me. My name is Dr Robinson. Dr Christopher Robinson. Will Mr Hound be joining us?'

'Mr 'Ound is out on an errand at the moment. Things 'ave been a bit 'ectic around these 'ere parts recently, Doctor,' replied Cornelius, turning his head and smiling warmly at two giant wolfhounds who were artfully positioned in the far corner of the room (one – the largest dog that Robinson had ever seen, with fur the colour of blackened flint – lying stretched across a long sofa like a pole-axed walrus, and the other – smaller, scruffier, and wheaten in colour, save for blood-red ears with the faintest hints of white spots upon them – sitting like an alert gargoyle and intently studying the patterns on the carpet).

'MARY MOTHER OF GOD!' yelped Doctor Robinson, leaping onto the seat of the armchair like a musophobic scullery maid noticing a mischievous mouse scurrying malevolently towards her. 'How on earth did I miss those monsters?'

'Calm yourself, Doctor,' chortled Cornelius. 'They've already eaten today.'

Doctor Robinson shot the old codger an alarmed look, but, on seeing the broad and friendly grin on the fearsome old fellow's whiskery visage, realised the foolishness of his reaction and gently positioned himself back into the more practical and traditional position of the experienced armchair user.

'The chap on the sofa is my good friend, Jeffries,' beamed Cornelius. 'An' the old boy with the eye-liner is – Ah, Missus Dobbs. Tea! Lovely. If you could put it down on this 'ere table, an' I'll pour it out when it's 'ad a chance to steep.'

Missus Dobbs placed a large silver tray – that carried teapot, two cups and saucers of the finest bone china, along with matching sugar bowl and creamer – on a small wooden table to the side of the Professor's armchair, and

11

then bimbled from the room, gnawing on her knuckles and throwing agitated and concerned glances towards the tea set as she left.

'Any'ow, Dr Robinson,' continued Cornelius, 'may I enquire on 'ow it is that you find yourself 'ere?'

'An old friend recommended you to me, Professor. Captain Alexander Milner. We were at school together, then served with the Royal Warwickshires. Stayed in touch ever since. Works for some secret government agency these days. MI7, I shouldn't wonder. Hush hush, and all that. Doesn't like to talk about it and I don't like to ask.'

'I'm sure you don't, young sir. So, what is it, exactly, that we can be doing for you? An' why is it, may I ask, that you find yourself in need of the unusual talents of *Lyons an' 'Ound Paranormal Investigation Agency?*'

The smartly-dressed young doctor went a little pale and then leant forward, rested his elbows on his knees, swallowed loudly, and looked like he was trying very hard not to be sick.

Cornelius took the opportunity to appraise the young fellow.

Dr Christopher Robinson must have been in his early-to-mid thirties but still managed to retain a youthful (one might be tempted to say "boyish") demeanour. Light blond hair, cut in the latest fashion – short back and sides, with a foppish fringe that was in constant need of being swept out of his bright blue eyes (one of which was, at present, more than a little pinkish). Those *baby blues* sparkled with an unshakable sense of propriety that suggested an upbringing of impeccable correctness. He was dressed, smartly, in a grey three-piece suit, white cotton shirt and grey neck-tie. All in all, he looked like a character from an English children's novel who had grown up to be all the things that his no-doubt thoroughly decent and thoroughly middle-class parents had ever hoped for.

But for all his outward appearance of respectability and well-to-do-ness, a nervous, agitated and unsettled energy seemed to seep from every pore – and it wasn't anything to do with the *Wodin-Poke*[1] that Missus Dobbs (and what an unexpected and wonderful find she was!) had just so expertly administered to him on Black Lion Lane. But then, considered Cornelius, so many chaps his age wore that same haunted expression, that same nervous agitation. And who could blame them, with what they'd seen and what they'd been through? Cornelius had himself been to the very doors of Hell (literally, on one bowel-loosening occasion, he was very sorry to say) but he doubted that he'd ever come close to what some of these poor fellows had experienced during what was now being called *The Great War*.

'Take your time, Doctor,' said Cornelius, warmly, carefully pouring them each a cup of tea.

The wheaten-coloured wolfhound lifted his great black nose, sniffed the air, arched an enquiring eyebrow, then tilted his massive head to one side and looked uneasily in Cornelius' direction.

Dr Robinson slowly sat upright again, took a deep breath, nodded, and attempted a grin.

'You must forgive me, Professor. Whatever must you think of me?'

Cornelius handed the young man a cup and saucer and winked.

'Son,' he said kindly, 'if I told you 'alf of what, an' 'oo, I've seen over the years – an' in what state they'd arrived in when they'd come through our doors – I don't think you'd even begin to believe me … an' I don't think that it would settle your nerves any, neither. So, whatever it is that you've done, seen or 'eard, well, it'd be a surprise if it was a surprise, if you get what I mean.'

Dr Robinson took a moment to decipher the old codger's words, brought cup and saucer close to his lips … and then thought better of it and gently placed them back onto the small table beside his armchair. He lifted his head and lanced Cornelius with a haunted glare.

'Professor Lyons, what I am about to tell you, as experienced a hand as you no doubt are, will, I have no doubt, shock you to the core. It is not my intent to horrify you, so please forgive me if my story offends you in any way.'

The giant yellow hound let out an enormous, and perhaps overly-loud, yawn.

Cornelius stifled a smile in the depths of his wondrous whiskers and looked grimly at the young doctor.

'I'm all ears, son,' he said, earnestly.

'I am,' began Dr Christopher Robinson, 'the psychiatric consultant for an experimental project concerned with the rehabilitation of war veterans who are considered – how best to put it? – unable to cope with the rigours of everyday life. It is a small institution, named *Five Hundred Acre Asylum*, set in the most beautiful woodlands imaginable. Ashdown Forest, to be exact. The men in my care are all exceptional in their own peculiar way. All excelled themselves in The War. All were highly decorated. But, for whatever reason, none of them has been able to make the adjustment back to civilian life and put the unutterable horrors that they undoubtedly saw and experienced into that safe and hidden space that is required of us all, if we are once again to rejoin "normal" society.

'My work is to help these men, to treat them with the respect that their wartime heroics deserve, to repay the debt that our country owes them. And, in time, it is my hope that they may be rehabilitated and reintroduced back into the everyday world.'

'A most admirable endeavour, Dr Robinson,' nodded Cornelius. 'So, what's 'appened?'

Dr Robinson, sighed and shook his head.

'Two months ago, two bodies were discovered outside the grounds of the asylum.'

'Terrible news indeed. Most shocking. An' just 'oo were these poor unfortunates?'

'At first it was impossible to tell, for both poor souls had been decapitated.'

'Decapitated, you say? Their 'eads cut off?'

'Oh no, Professor. Not cut off – *pulled off*!'

'Crikey!'

'Their skulls were discovered some time later, and at some distance from the crime. And to make matters worse their ... their ...'

'Go on, son.'

'Their brains had been ... *removed*.'

'*Removed*, you say. 'Ow dreadful!'

'Both men turned out to be farmhands from the nearby village of Coleman's Hatch.'

'An' you believe that it were one of your inmates what 'ad gone back on the warpath, so to speak?'

'*Patients*, Professor, not *inmates*. And, no, most definitely not. All of our patients are kept under lock and key and under constant observation. There is not the slightest possibility that they could have escaped.'

'An' you're quite sure about that?'

'Most sure, yes.'

'An' what 'ave the police 'ad to say about the matter?'

'An investigation was conducted, of course, but no progress was made. The motive for the murders remains a mystery. And as to the execution of such a horrible attack, well, we are all at a loss, for what manner of man, I ask you, would possess the strength to pull another man's head clean from his shoulders?'

'Hhhmmm?' hhhmmmed Cornelius, wiggling his whiskers.

'But worse was to follow,' continued Dr Robinson, with a miserable shake of his head that sent his fringe tumbling into his eyes. 'Last month another two bodies were discovered on the very same spot. Both murdered in the same horrendous manner – their heads ripped from their shoulders. And when their heads were finally found, their brains had too been plucked from their skulls.'

'More local farm'ands?' enquired Cornelius, sounding both curious and appalled.

Dr Robinson shook his head and took a deep breath. 'No,' he replied. 'Two of the asylum's porters, I'm most sorry to say.'

'Well, that is shocking news indeed, Dr Robinson. An' just what 'ave the rozzers 'ad to say about all this?'

'The *rozzers*?'

'The police, Dr Robinson. The police.'

'Ah. Yes. I see. Well, they seem to be truly baffled, as are we all. And furthermore, I'm extremely sorry to have to say that they appear to be thoroughly disinterested in the whole grisly affair. Extraordinary! You'd have thought that four foul murders committed in the heart of the peaceful Sussex countryside would cause quite a stir among the local constabulary, but, I'm forced to conclude, they appear to be alarmingly unconcerned. However, that's all by the by. As you can imagine, myself and my staff are living in dread, what with the full moon being only a few days away.'

'Full moon?' asked Cornelius, an eyebrow tilting to an intrigued and curious angle.

The wheaten wolfhound pricked up his ears and wound his head forward.

'Why, yes. Did I forget to mention that both sets of murders were committed on the night of the full moon?'

'You did, Dr Robinson, you did, an' most intriguing it is,' purred Professor Lyons.

'That is why I find myself seeking your advice on the matter, Professor. When I met up with Millie ... oh, excuse me, I mean Captain Milner, at our old boys' reunion the other day, I was discussing the horrendous affair with him and I must say that he grew most interested. Advised me to keep it under my hat, but he said that he'd see if his department would take a look into it. Then I had a telephone call from him yesterday morning saying that they didn't have the resources at the moment to spare any of their chaps, but that I should contact the esteemed paranormal investigation agency of *Lyons and Hound* to see if it was something that might be of interest to you. He recommended you most highly, I must say.'

'So you believe it to be a matter of the paranormal?' asked Cornelius.

Dr Robinson gnawed his lips. 'Who knows, Professor? Who knows? But I'm prepared to look into the possibility. I was at Mons[2], you know. I saw things that ... well ... that are outside the understanding of rational science. God damn it, man! *"There are more things in heaven and earth, Horatio,"* and all that. And besides, more lives may be at stake. I'll pursue whatever lead I can to get to the bottom of this dreadful mess, Professor Lyons, no matter what the cost.'

Professor Lyons stroked his whiskers thoughtfully, whilst looking over to the giant hounds. 'All right. I tell you what, Dr Robinson, we'll drop by your gaff as soon as we can an' take a peek.'

'A great kindness, Professor. Thank you. I have directions to Five Hundred Acre Asylum here,' he said, pulling a folded sheet of paper from the pocket of his jacket, 'plus a telephone number that I can be contacted on. My word! Is that the time?' he cried, looking at his watch and leaping from his chair. 'So sorry, must dash. I'll be late for my afternoon appointments. I'll make my own way out. And once again, thank you, Professor.'

TWO
Questions

When Dr Robinson had left, Cornelius turned and looked at the great wheaten-coloured wolfhound, who had lifted his wiry backside from the carpet and was ambling purposefully towards the enormous armchair. Despite being used to the unearthly sight (not the wiry backside but the shape-shifting transformation), Dandy Lyons couldn't help but raise an astounded eyebrow as a five-second cacophony of cracks and pops (like popcorn popping in a covered pan) rippled through the room, and there before him stood the terrifying form of the seven-and-a-half foot tall were-wolf-wolfhound, known (fearfully) throughout The Nine Realms as *The Hound Who Hunts Nightmares*. Reaching quickly for his red silk dressing-gown, the were-hound hastily dressed (while Cornelius politely averted his gaze), leant down and enthusiastically sniffed the great seat that Dr Robinson had been occupying, then turned and looked at his friend, companion and business partner with the look of the hunter sparkling in his walnut-coloured and almond-shaped eyes.

'So, what do you think, 'Aitch?' asked Cornelius, reaching over to pick up cup and saucer from the side table, and rest it in the palm of his shovel-like mitt.

The were-wolfhound settled himself into his armchair, flared his nostrils, arched a bushy eyebrow and pierced Cornelius with a mystified gaze.

'I'm not sure that I've ever smelt its like. Just what, in the name of all the Gods and their unholy mothers, is it?'

Cornelius looked a little confused for a moment, then followed The Hound's enquiring gaze towards the teacup and saucer that he held. He gave it a tentative sniff. 'Tea ... I 'ope. Well, that's what I asked for at any rate. Must be some kind of new imported leaf or some such ... *thing.*'

'Well, go on, man, give it a sip,' egged the were-wolfhound, eyeing the cup and saucer that rested on the table next to him with a look of barely-concealed suspicion.

Cornelius squinted doubtfully into the cup, wiggled his whiskers uncertainly, and then looked up at his friend's inquisitive visage. 'I was talking about Dr Robinson,' he blustered, hastily setting the teacup and saucer back onto the table. 'Well? What do you think?'

'What, indeed? Most mystifying. A brace of double murders, both committed on the night of a full moon. All the victims murdered in the same macabre manner; decapitated by someone, or *something*, of quite exceptional strength – or, perhaps, by mechanical means – and then their brains removed. Well, there can be little doubt that something untoward is taking place, and quite possibly of a supernatural nature. I suspect some kind of ghastly ritual. Satanic, perhaps Druidic. What say you, Dandy?'

'Buggered if I know,' sniffed the tweedy old duffer. 'So, what say you, that we pop straight down to this 'ere Five 'Undred Acre Asylum an' 'ave a gander?'

'Capital idea, my dear fellow. Was going to suggest that very thing. But before we do, I think a telephone call is in order. A telephone call to one Special Agent Alexander Milner of *The Unseen League.*[3] Sound chap, Milner. I've met him on a number of occasions. Was the rising star of *The League* a few years ago, before that unfortunate incident with Gertie the Grindylow took the sheen off his promising career. These kind of things never tend to work out, as well you know, dear chap. '

Cornelius muttered something into his Newgate Knocker as The Hound pushed himself from his armchair and jauntily trotted over to the candlestick telephone that was half-hidden under the piles of books and files that were scattered over the large writing-desk at the far end of The Study.

'Operator, could you please put me through to Dylan and Don's Fishmongers.[4] London, Pimlico ... Yes, I'll wait.'

The Hound pressed the mouthpiece to his chest and looked over to Cornelius with what might have been a smile. 'What intrigues me,' he mused, licking the tip of an enormous canine with the tip of his enormous tongue, 'is why *The League* aren't involving themselves in whatever is going on at Five Hundred Acre Asylum. And why Agent Milner was so keen for poor Dr Robinson to seek our help. It makes me wonder just wh– Ah, good morning ... Yes, I was hoping that I could speak to Captain Milner ... No, he's not expecting my call, but it is rather urgent ... Is he, indeed? If you could please tell him that it's Mr Percival Percy, I'm sure that he'll be able to find some time ... Thank you ... Yes, of course. Most kind.'

The Hound pressed the mouthpiece of the phone against his chest once more.

'As I was saying,' he continued, 'just why are *The League* so disinterested? And why, if the good doctor is to be believed, have the police been so lacklustre in their investigations into what are surely a most shocking and heinous set of crimes?'

'Maybe they just 'aven't got the manpower,' grumbled Cornelius, chewing his whiskers and eyeing his teacup like a chary owl.

The were-hound snorted. 'Four homicides in the same location and the police do nothing? Four gruesome murders with a possible occult or supernatural leaning and *The Unseen League* (whose very raison d'être is the investigation into crimes of a supernatural persuasion) refuse to send anyone to investigate? No, Dandy. Whatever is going on, it smells a little fishy, if you ask me – Ah! Captain Milner. How very good of you to spare the time, I do understand how busy you must be ...'

20

THREE
The Achilles Project

Captain Alexander Milner got off the train at the newly-completed Tunbridge Wells Central Railway Station, decided against hailing a cab, and began the half a mile hike to The White Horse public house. Walking even such a short distance was no easy matter for the Captain, and he was forced to lean heavily on his stick as he limped his way along Mount Pleasant Road, but he had long ago made the decision that he would not let his injury (picked up at the Somme, though he didn't like to talk about it) dictate what he should and shouldn't (and could and couldn't) do. Besides, he was early for his appointment and there was no need to rush. It was a fine morning and he needed, and rather looked forward to, the exercise.

The landlord of The White Horse, Mr John Steadman, waited patiently for Milner to climb the stairs, before ushering him along the hallway and leading him to a plain wooden door that had clearly seen better days.

'Professor Lyons is in here, sir,' he said, letting the Captain regain his breath after his exertions. 'And I do hope you're a dog-lover,' he grinned, ''cos he's got a flipping monster with him! The damned thing's the size of a bloody pony, it is.'

Steadman made to open the door, but Milner shot out a hand and stayed him.

'I can take it from here, my good man,' he smiled. 'Thank you.'

The publican muttered something about 'only trying to help', and made his way back down the hall and to the bar, no doubt to gossip to his regulars about the strange goings-on that were taking place in his respectable establishment.

Milner waited for him to disappear down the stairs and then knocked on the door.

There was a short pause before a gruff voice replied, ''Ello?'

'It's Milner. Captain Milner.'

There was another short pause, and what sounded like a piece of heavy furniture being moved away from the threshold, before the handle turned and the door was prised open a little. A badger-like head seeped through the gap and eyed Milner up and down.

''Ow do, Captain. Glad you could make it. You all right, son? You look a little peaky.'

'I'm fine, thank you. Professor Lyons, I presume?'

'At your service, sir,' beamed Cornelius, opening the door a little wider. 'Well, don't just stand there, come on in, son. Come on in.'

Captain Milner squeezed himself past the cast iron bulk of Professor Lyons, turned and took the old fellow's outstretched paw, and found his own rather slender hand engulfed in a mitt that looked like it had been chiselled (badly) out of seasoned oak.

Professor Lyons looked like no professor that Milner had ever seen (and, believe me, he'd seen more than his fair share of eccentric academics during his stint at Trinity College). For even though the old fellow was dapperly dressed in a somewhat outdated three-piece tweed suit, and even though he sported a somewhat astonishing and rather old-fashioned set of whiskers (not uncommon among certain of the more ancient lecturers who had haunted the Captain's university days), the man was built like a heavyweight boxing champion, and his presence would have been more than a little menacing if it weren't for the kindly twinkle in his eyes. Milner had come across that look only a few times before, and for all that it was a

22

comfort, it was also more than a little disturbing, for that particular sort of *kindly twinkle* came only from a place of absolute confidence in the owner's ability to handle themselves in any given situation. Milner instantly placed Professor Lyons in the *"dangerous individual, not to be gotten on the wrong side of - department"*, and turned to see just where Mr Percy might be.

Seated in the far end of the room sat *The Hound Who Hunts Nightmares* himself, dressed in a tweed overcoat with the collars turned up, and with a baker boy hat perched on his head at a rather jaunty angle.

'Ah, Captain Milner,' he said, with what might have been an attempt at a smile, his voice impossibly deep and impossibly plummy. 'How very good of you to make it. And how very good to see you again, my dear fellow.'

Professor Lyons returned to the room carrying a tray with two pints of bitter, a bowl of water and a small pile of steak and ale pies stacked upon it. He placed the tray on the table where The Hound and Milner were sitting, re-wedged an armchair back up against the door handle, and then joined his companions.

'Your very good 'ealth, gentlemen,' he winked, raising his glass and then taking a long draught of ale, leaving an impressive moustache of foam on his impressive moustache of whiskers. 'So, where were we, then?'

The were-hound looked at the bowl of water with a disdainful curl of his lip, and then plucked up a pie.

'Captain Milner was explaining his concerns over what might be happening at Five Hundred Acre Asylum,' he said, carefully examining the pie before snaffling it down in one mouthful.

'Indeed,' sighed Milner, taking a sip of bitter and rather nervously watching the were-hound's impressive gnashers as he devoured another of the delicious-looking pastries. 'To be honest, I've not a shred of evidence to back up my fears, but things seem to be a little *untoward*, if you ask me.'

'*Untoward*, son?' asked Cornelius, fondly fondling a second pie.

'Well, yes. When Chris – Dr Robinson – first told me what had happened at the asylum, I felt sure that it would be of great interest to *The League*. And so, at the very first opportunity, I reported the incident to my superiors.'

'And what did they have to say about the matter?' enquired The Hound, casually snatching up another pastry from the tray.

'Well, that was what really piqued my interest, Mr Percy, because I was told, in no uncertain manner, that I should keep my nose out of it, and that it was none of *The League's* business.'

'Unusual,' sniffed the were-hound, licking gravy from the tips of his claws.

'I may not be the flavour of the month at the moment, not after the ... after the ... the *incident* ...'

'Gertie?' offered Cornelius, manfully munching on a steak and ale-filled delight.

'Quite,' replied Milner, reddening in the face a little, '... but – well, for God's sake! – that's what *The League* is all about, isn't it? A series of heinous crimes are committed that smack of an occult leaning, to say the very least, and we're told to look the other way and twiddle our thumbs. It's not right, I tell you.'

'And so ...?' asked The Hound, tapping his nose with the last of the pastries, as Cornelius looked on forlornly.

'And so I did a little digging off my own bat, you might say. Probably get myself into all sorts of bother, but, well, let's just say that my time in *The League's* employment might be coming to an end sooner rather than later. '

'What did you find, Captain?'

'Well, Mr Percy, not much, *but* ...' Milner took a deep breath, cast his eyes around the room and then leant in a little closer, 'it would appear that Five Hundred Acre Asylum *is* very much on *The League's* list of *"interesting things to keep an eye on"*, so to speak. And it looks very much to me like the military have got their sticky little hands all over it. Some hushed whispers about something called "The Achilles Project". Can't tell you any more than that, but I'd take a guess and say that Five Hundred Acre Asylum is being used to test some sort of weapon, and, if *The Unseen League* is involved, that weapon must be of a supernatural bent.'

'But if that were the case, Captain, then surely Dr Robinson would have told us as much?' suggested The Hound.

Milner shook his head. 'Not necessarily. Chris only works with the inmates during office hours. Come five o'clock, rain or shine, he's ushered from the premises. As far as his superiors are concerned he's there to assess his patients and help them rehabilitate, nothing more, nothing less. Whatever goes on after dark is seen as none of his business.'

'Intriguing,' sighed The Hound, with a smack of his lips, looking disparagingly towards the water bowl and then eyeing Cornelius's half-downed pint with a look of barely-concealed envy. 'I think that it's high time that we paid Five Hundred Acre Asylum a little visit, don't you, Dandy?'

'That I do, 'Aitch, that I do,' smiled Cornelius, draining his glass and wiping his moustache on the back of his hand. He pulled a weighty hunter from his waistcoat pocket and checked the time. 'A three 'our 'ike an' we'll be there just in time for our little rendezvous with Dr Robinson at The Gallipot Inn. Fancy joining us, Captain?'

Milner gently tapped his leg with his walking stick. 'Wish that I could, chaps,' he smiled ruefully. 'But this old pin of mine just won't hold up to that sort of punishment these days, I'm most sorry to say. Besides, I'd better get myself back to the office or they might start asking questions. If they ever find out that I've been here with you there'll be all Hell to pay. Let me do a little more digging about. Give me a call at the office later on this evening and I'll let you know if I've been able to unearth anything more.'

With no little effort Captain Milner hauled himself from his chair and extended his hand, first to Cornelius and then, a little tentatively, to The Hound.

'Good luck, Mr Percy, Professor. And Godspeed. And you will keep an eye out for Chris, won't you? He is such a dear, dear friend.'

As he closed the door behind him Milner heard the clipped tones of the were-wolf-wolfhound. 'Thanks awfully for the lend of the threads, old man. Much appreciated,' followed by a five-second cacophony of cracks and pops (like popcorn popping in a closed saucepan) and then the gruff voice of the Professor muttering something about dog hairs all over his favourite coat.

FOUR
The Gallipot Inn

They met Dr Christopher Robinson in the garden of The Gallipot Inn in Hartfield, just in time for a little spot of something for supper.

'Where's Mr Hound, Professor?' asked Dr Robinson, looking a little disappointed (and eyeing The Hound – though he didn't know that *this* hound was in fact *the* The Hound – with a chary respect).

''E'll be down tomorrow, Doctor, in time for the full moon. Let's 'ope we can catch the murderous rascals before they commit another 'einous atrocity. That's if they's going to try it again, that is, 'ooever the rotten so-an'-sos might be,' replied Cornelius, casting an expert eye over the dinnertime 'specials' menu that was chalked on the pub's outdoor blackboard.

'I say,' chortled the young doctor, 'this magnificent fellow isn't Mr Hound, is he?' Dr Robinson nodded his head subtly in the direction of the mighty yellow wolfhound (who *was*, in fact, Mr Hound, but was trying very hard not to look like he might be) almost as if he didn't want to offend the colossal canine.

The wiry wheaten giant, who appeared (if one didn't know better) to have been eyeing the dinnertime 'specials' menu with a look that suggested a forlorn and longing regret, suddenly turned and caught Dr Robinson's eye, then swiftly looked away and let out a loud yawn, followed by an ear-splitting trump, before lowering himself into a resting position.

'Most amusing, Doctor,' chuckled Cornelius. ''E's got a good nose, 'as this one. Bring 'im along on a case or two, now an' then. Can sniff a wrong'un a mile off. An' 'e's 'andy to 'ave around if there 'appens to be any bother, if you get my drift.'

'I bet he is,' cooed Christopher Robinson, tentatively stretching out a hand to pat The Hound on the head and then thinking better of it as the wolfhound curled a thin black lip to reveal a fleeting glimpse of a truly terrifying set of gnashers. 'What's his name? Jeffries was the other one, wasn't it? Where's he?'

The Hound hauled himself to his feet and sauntered over to take a drink of water from the dog bowl by the pub door.

'My good friend Jeffries is back at One Punch Cottage, 'olding the fort, so to speak, with Missus Dobbs.'

'So what's this fine fellow's name, then?'

'Err ... 'e's called ... er ... erhm ... *Scruffy*(?).'

Dr Robinson's good-natured response of 'How delightful!' was lost in the sudden sound of an enormous wheaten-coloured sighthound choking into a water bowl.

'*Mister* Scruffy,' sniffed Cornelius, hurriedly (and perhaps a little apologetically).

'So, Professor,' said the Doctor, turning his gaze from the hacking hound and piercing Cornelius with a look of serious intent, 'have you any theories as to just what might be going on over at Five Hundred Acre Woods?'

'Well, Doctor, we 'ave 'eard a rumour that the military might be involved in this small, experimental, an' rather secretive project of yours. Is that right?'

Dr Robinson caught the eye of the landlady, who had just popped out to clear up some empty glasses. 'That's no secret, Professor. The director of the faculty is one Major Wolbury. Supposedly a brilliant mind, they say. Glittering career, and all that. Though if you ask me the man appears to be nothing short of a blithering buffoon. Without wishing to sound rude, I'd say the old fellow was far too weak-willed and uncertain of himself to be in charge of such a cutting-edge project. But, hey-ho, who am I to judge? Ah, the lovely Miss Sands! And how are you this fine afternoon? How about a couple of your delicious leek and chicken tarts? That all right, Professor? Splendid. Two pints of Best, as well, please, Annie. And any chance of an old bone for the big fellow over there? Thanks, Annie, you're a brick.'

Cornelius waited for the landlady of The Gallipot Inn to walk away before leaning in a little closer.

'So you ain't 'eard nothing about something called "The Achilles Project", then?' he enquired.

The Hound, recovering from his coughing fit, ambled back and sat a little behind Dr Robinson.

'*Achilles Project*, you say? At Five Hundred Acre Asylum? No. Can't say that I have. What is it?'

The Hound began to scratch himself in a staccato fashion.

'I was 'oping that you might be able to 'elp us out on that one, Doctor, what with you working there, an' all.'

'I haven't got the faintest idea, I'm afraid. Though to be honest, all of us *civilian-Johnnies* are ushered out of the building at five o'clock on the dot.'

'That's what we 'eard from Captain Milner. Bit fishy, don't you think?'

'You spoke to Alex?'

Cornelius nodded.

'I see. And what does he have to say? ... I say!' Christopher Robinson spun around and stared at The Hound in astonishment.

'Whatever is it, Doctor?'

Doctor Robinson shook his head, flicked his fringe out of his eyes, and chuckled. 'I must be going mad,' he chortled, turning back around to smile sheepishly at the tweedy old bruiser seated before him. 'For a moment I could have sworn that your dog was scratching himself in Morse Code!'

The Hound shot Cornelius a mortified gurn from behind Robinson's back and hastily scratched at his ear like a thing possessed.

Cornelius sighed into his whiskers. 'If 'e was, I'd sell 'im to the circus in a jiffy. Time for the old fellow to 'ave a bath, I think. Ain't that right, you silly old fleabag? You an expert on Morse Code, Doctor?'

'Short stint with the Royal Corps of Signals. But no expert, by any means.'

'So,' so-ed Cornelius, hastily changing the subject, 'just 'ow do we go about finding what's what an' 'oo's oo up at the asylum, then? Any chance you can get me in to 'ave a look around?'

'I'm a step ahead of you on that one, Professor,' winked the Doctor. 'I've laid the foundation for the ruse that my old university mentor is coming down to help me go through some case notes tomorrow morning. Nobody's even questioned it. Didn't bat an eyelid. Old Wol-Wol (that's Major Wolbury to you) was all for it, in fact. My assistant, Dr Coney's nose was put out of joint a bit, but then when isn't it, I ask you? Got your pass right here. You're to be one *Professor Isaiah Tinkle.*'

They both stared at The Hound, who had snorted loudly and was now desperately fixing his attention on something on the far horizon while his lips fidgeted most alarmingly.

'The real Tinkle's a bit older than you, and halfway to the loony bin by all accounts (poor old Tinky) but you'll pass, I'm sure. And who's going to bother to check, anyway?'

'Charmed,' sniffed Cornelius.

'I say, Professor? Just what are you a professor of, anyway?'

'That's a long conversation, son.'

'I see. Well, old Tinkle is ... was ... is an expert in the field of *abnormal and unusual personality disorders*, just in case anybody asks.'

'Right up my alley,' groaned Cornelius.

30

'Anyhow, there's an abandoned old shepherd's hut on the edge of the woods. No one ever goes there. To be honest, I doubt that anybody even knows it exists. I've set you up a bed and a small stove, plus left you a few days' supplies; a couple of Annie's scrumptious pies, a loaf of bread and some cheese, and a bottle of port (just in case).'

'That's very kind of you, Doctor.'

'A great pleasure. Should be a cosy little bunk for you and your friend.'

'Friend?'

'Scruffy.'

'Scruffy. Yes, yes of course.'

'Dogs aren't allowed on the asylum's grounds, so you'll have to keep him out of sight for the time being, I'm afraid.'

'Not a problem, Doctor. You won't 'ear a peep out of 'im, you 'ave my word on it. Now, is there any chance that I can take a look at the scene of the murders before it gets too dark?'

'Yes, of course. We'll drop your stuff off at the hut, lock Scruffy in – just so he doesn't get himself into any mischief (we don't want the locals thinking that there's a monster on the loose, now, do we?) – and then head straight there.' Dr Robinson gnawed his lip and then swept his fringe from his eyes. 'So, correct me if I'm wrong, Professor, but you think that these dreadful killings might be an inside job? Committed by someone at the asylum? Somehow connected to this – what was it you called it? – *Achilles Project*?'

''Oo knows, Doctor Robinson, 'oo knows. But it's the one lead that we 'ave, so it'd be fool'ardy not to follow it up. Might be nothing, but we've got to start somewhere.'

'Indeed. I suppose we do.' Dr Robinson paused and then sniffed and rubbed his nose thoughtfully, 'Just an idea, but if there *is* anything untoward going on at Five Hundred Acre, I think Gibbet is the fellow to ask.'

'Sorry, son, I think I mis'eard you.'

31

'Gibbet,' smiled Dr Robinson. 'He's one of the orderlies at the asylum.'

'That's one 'ell of a moniker 'e's got there.'

'Ha ha! His real name is Bertie Troynt –'

'That's almost worse.'

'– but everybody calls him *Gibbet*. Funny little fellow. Most odd. Become a bit of a favourite with the staff. Seems to have made himself invaluable. I did hear a rumour that he started out as a patient, though God alone knows what he was doing there, the poor fellow's as timid as a mouse. Anyway, he's about the only non-military-type who works both the day and the night shift. If anyone were to know anything, he might just be our very best bet. I'll make sure that you get to meet with him tomorrow. Ah ha! Here comes the lovely Annie with her delicious leek and chicken tarts. We'll wolf these down, Professor, and then I'll take you to your lodgings. What's that, Annie? No bones for the big fellow. Ah well, looks like poor old Mister Scruffy is just going to have to go hungry.'

FIVE
Posingford Wood

As the sun began to slowly dip in the sky, Dr Christopher Robinson led Professor Cornelius Lyons/*Professor Isaiah Tinkle* and Mr Hound/*Scruffy* down Gallipot Hill, along Cotchfield Lane and finally into the cathedral-like stillness of Posingford Wood. Leaving the path, they followed after Dr Robinson as he picked his way through the towering trees until, at last, they came to a low and crumbling flint wall that was all but buried beneath a tumbling mass of vines and brambles.

Dr Robinson looked over his shoulder, as if he suspected that they might be being watched, and then hurdled the wall with surprising agility. Cornelius rolled The Hound a *look*, and then followed. The Hound sniffed the air and then licked his teeth before seeping over the wall like a wiry golden shadow.

Within a few strides they found themselves standing before an old shepherd's hut (essentially, a big garden shed on wheels). (Of course there was no way of knowing if the previous inhabitant of said hut was in any way of advanced years, but it was an undeniable fact that the building had certainly seen many, and better, days.) Dr Robinson cast a sheepish smile at his companions, pulled a key from his pocket and unlocked the hut's stable door, then leaped up into the darkness of the wooden structure (the hut's floor being a few feet above the ground). Within seconds Dr Robinson poked his head back through the doorway.

'Well don't just stand there, old chap! Come and have a look at your new lodgings,' he grinned.

Cornelius plucked his baker boy cap from his grizzled head, pulled his nose and then hauled himself up into the hut.

The hut was made up of a single room and was furnished with a small wooden table (with two matching chairs tucked under it, and on which stood a bag full of the provisions that Dr Robinson had promised), a battered stove, and two camp beds pushed head-to-head against adjacent walls.

'Sorry about the meagre furnishings, Professor, but it was the best that I could rustle up at such short notice.'

'Known worse,' smiled the tweedy old codger. 'In fact, it takes me back a few years, if truth be told. Come on, *Scruffy*, up you come, lad.'

The Hound briefly curled a thin black lip in disdain, then sighed, sprang into the shack and made a great show of making himself comfortable on the larger of the two beds.

'So, Dr Robinson,' continued Cornelius, offering the wolfhound a withering gurn, 'best we 'ead off an' take a peek at that there murder scene, afore it gets too dark, wouldn't you say?'

'Yes, yes of course. Let's lock Mr Scruffy in here and then I'll take you right there.'

'Cracking,' smiled Cornelius.

And off they set.

Within a hundred strides Cornelius pulled up short.

'Damn it!' he huffed. 'Can I 'ave the key from you, Doctor. I think I left my torch back at the 'ut.'

Back at the hut, Cornelius unlocked the door to find The Hound (in were-form) helping himself to one of Miss Sand's scrumptious steak and mushroom pies.

'Absolutely famished, old stick,' he grinned, as he took a bracing swig of port.

''Ere, you better leave some of that for me, *Mr Scruffy*, or there'll be all 'Ell to pay.'

'Don't you worry about that, *Professor Tinkle*, my dear fellow,' replied the were-hound, as he munched on with great delight. 'Go along with Robinson and see what you can make of it all. I'll give you a few minutes' start before I head off and take a scout about on my own. Whistle a couple of bars of *"The Spaniard That Blighted My Life"*[5] to give me the heads up if the doctor is with you when you return. Good hunting, old friend. And see if you can get to a public phone and give Milner a call, will you? Hopefully the Captain might have some more news for us.'

With one last lingering look at the pie and the port, Cornelius tipped his cap and hurried off to catch up with Dr Robinson.

Dr Robinson and Cornelius stumped their way through the trees until they reached the edge of the forest. They stopped at a slow-running stream that chortled with a lazy wisdom beneath a rickety wooden bridge. Christopher Robinson marched onto the bridge, leant against the railings and looked along the river's meandering course.

'The bodies were all found snagged at that bend in the river,' he mused mournfully, pointing towards the spot. 'Their heads were found on Gills Lap.'

'Gill's lap! 'Oo's that?'

'It's a small hill, Professor, at the very top of the forest. There's a circle of trees at its summit, sixty-three of them ... or is it sixty-four? Damned if I can remember. Enchanting place. Most enchanting. Well, it was. Not sure if I'll ever be able to disassociate it from this horrible affair now.'

'Enchanting, you say?' purred Dandy, lifting his hat and running his fingertips through his grizzled hair.

'Gills Lap is about an hour's hike from here, so I don't think that we'll have time to take a proper look before we lose the light.'

Cornelius joined Christopher Robinson on the bridge and peered over towards the bend in the river, before trotting across and over to the spot where the poor souls' headless corpses had gathered. He looked up in time to see The Hound (in wolfhound form) in the distance, slipping like a golden whisper through the trees and away towards Gills Lap.

'Anything else you can tell me, Doctor?' he asked, looking over towards Robinson. The doctor, oblivious to the were-hound's presence, shook his head glumly.

Cornelius stuck his hands in his pockets and studied the darkening sky.

'Then I suppose we better 'ead off. 'Ere, I don't suppose that there's a public telephone that I could use before we call it a night, is there, Doctor?'

The sun had long since retreated from the sky when Cornelius returned to the old shepherd's hut. To his absolute delight he found The Hound already there, making short work of the cheese and punishing the port with a look of happy relish plastered on his wiry visage.

'Ah, Dandy! There you are, dear chap. I was beginning to think that you and Robinson had decamped yourselves back at The Gallipot and had forgotten about poor old Mr Scruffy altogether. Shocking! A poor fellow might starve to death, you know. Some people just shouldn't be allowed to have a dog licence, if you ask me.'

'Looks like the old mutt is doing more than all right for 'isself,' grimaced Cornelius, looking at the diminishing block of cheddar and the bottle of port (currently clutched in the were-hound's mighty paw) with dismay.

'Oh, do sit down!' sighed the were-wolf-wolfhound, as he flashed a cheeky smile at his friend, then poured a hefty measure of port into a battered tin cup and pushed it towards the old fellow.

Cornelius pulled up a chair and took a swig.

'Ah! Aqua Corinthia!' he sighed, as he drained his cup dry and then poured himself and The Hound another measure.

'So then, 'Aitch, find anything that might be useful?'

The were-hound tapped his talons against the rim of his battered tin cup and licked his lips thoughtfully.

'Nothing that would hold up in court,' he mused. 'But it seems to me that there might be the suggestion of some rather unusual tracks up on Gills Lap.'

'*Unusual*? 'Ow so?'

'Clawed. Like a badger's ... only bigger.'

'A badger's, you say?'

'Perhaps. Hard to say with any certainty. The whole place is awash with the clumping great footprints of a gaggle of regulation size ten boots. '

'That'd be the rozzers.'

'Indeed. Plus, whatever other tracks *are* up there they were clearly made some weeks ago.'

'A month ago, per'aps?' pondered Cornelius, eyeing the cheese-block like a famished vole in mourning. 'Around about the time of the last full moon?'

The Hound wrinkled his nose.

'So,' growled Cornelius, – 'ooh, ta very much,' – he cackled, as The Hound pushed the block of cheddar towards him, 'are you suggesting that we're looking at some sort of were-beast, a *child of the moon*, being responsible for these 'ere murders?'

'Four bodies found on the nights of a full moon, their heads *pulled* from their shoulders by something of superhuman strength ... It does appear to lead us in that direction.'

'A were-badger, do you think? Ever 'eard of such a thing, 'Aitch?'

'Thankfully not,' snorted the were-hound. 'What about you, old chap? Learn anything more from Doctor Robinson?'

'No. Nothing new. 'Owever, I did manage to speak to Captain Milner.'

'Good show, old man. And did the fine Captain have anything to add to our understanding of this whole scurrilous affair?'

'Well,' sniffed Cornelius, tearing off a chunk of bread and wrapping it carefully around a hefty hunk of cheddar, ''e did a little more digging about, as 'e promised 'e would, an' 'e seems to think that this Major Wolbury might be at the bottom of things. It appears that 'e was the one what put the stop on any in-depth investigations by the police or *The League*. Apparently 'e's got friends in 'igh places, so to speak. So 'igh, it's rumoured, that you'd give yourself a flippin' nosebleed just trying to get an introduction.'

'Is that so?' purred The Hound, plucking up the bottle of port and pouring them both another generous measure. '"High places" in *The League*, or further afield?'

'Further afield. Pretty much got 'isself *carte blanche*, if the rumours are true, that is.'

'So that would imply that he's no longer acting under *The League's* directives? But this *Achilles Project*, that *is The Unseen League's* venture, yes?'

'It seem *likely*, 'Aitch, but 'e can't say with any certainty. But just as to *what* it actually is, no one seems to know. Or, at least, no one's telling Milner. But it would appear that this Wolbury fellow might 'ave gone beyond the pale, as it were. Or at least beyond 'is orders from *The Unseen League's* 'eadquarters. If it is them what's be'ind the whole affair, that is.'

'Fascinating. Well then, my old friend, tomorrow, come what may, make sure you get the chance to have a little *tête-à-tête* with this Major Wolbury chappie.'

'Consider it done, 'Aitch,' smiled Cornelius, raising his tin cup to the were-hound.

'In the morning I'll take another look around for any further signs of *untoward* activity. All being well, we'll rendezvous back here at lunchtime to catch up on any progress that might have been made. And then, come the evening, the game is afoot in earnest!' he cried, the bright light of the hunter sparkling in his almond-shaped and walnut-coloured eyes as he raised his vessel.

They clinked battered tin cups together.

''Ere's to your good 'ealth, my friend. An' 'appy 'unting.'

SIX
A Dandy In The Asylum

Nurse Rooney looked up from the reception desk to see the lovely Dr Robinson escorting what she could best describe as a henchman from a Victorian crime novel – wearing the loudest tweed suit she'd seen this side of the Drury Lane music halls, with shoulders like a navvy and whiskers like a baited ferret – through the front door of the Five Hundred Acre Asylum.

'Good morning, Kate,' smiled Dr Robinson, with boyish good charm. 'How's the little fellow? Recovering from his misadventures, I hope.' (Nurse Rooney's little lad had recently been taken quite ill after falling in the River Cuckmere whilst on a family picnic.)

'He's doing fine, thank you for asking, Dr Robinson,' smiled Nurse Rooney, her voice betraying a slight colonial twang. She turned her attentions to the imposing figure of the tweed-encased bruiser standing next to him (currently hovering like a badly-shaved grizzly bear stuffed into a Haymarket pimp's finest threads) and the smile puckered on her face.

'Oh. How rude of me. Nurse Rooney,' oozed Dr Robinson, 'this is Professor Isaiah Tinkle ... my old mentor ... from my university days ... in Oxford. A leading light in his ... my ... our field. He's kindly offered to go through some of the more ... *interesting* ... case studies with me. It's been given the all-clear by Major Wolbury,' he blathered, with what Cornelius considered to be an alarming display of nervous over-eagerness.

Nurse Rooney eyed *Professor Tinkle* like a brooding moorhen watching a dancing weasel.

Cornelius offered his most scholarly smile.

"Ow do,' he grinned, shooting the horse-faced nurse a most unscholarly wink.

Nurse Rooney, with a 3/10 attempt to mask her astonished disbelief that this rather baleful (and, to her mind, somewhat unsavoury-looking) individual could be in possession of anything approaching a mind of academic excellence, pulled her attention away from the loudly-dressed gorilla standing rather awkwardly before her and to the jet-black leather diary on her desk. She plucked open the journal with a talon-like nail and scanned down the day's entries.

After what felt like a short eternity, the diary was snapped shut with a brutal finality that made both Dr Robinson and Professor Lyons/Tinkle jump.

'Good morning, Professor,' she beamed, the smile on her face flowering again like a rehydrating prune. 'Lovely to have you aboard. Would you mind signing the visitors book before Dr Robinson takes you to his office?'

Dr Robinson led Cornelius past the burly orderly standing by the interior doors (who, Cornelius couldn't help but note, had all the bearing of a military guardsman doing his very best to look like he'd never even seen the inside of a barracks, let alone gone through any sort of advanced training – and failing with a rather admirable aplomb), along a rather soulless corridor and into a small, musty-smelling room that passed as his (Robinson's) office.

Dr Robinson gently closed the door behind them and let out a deep breath.

'Well, that's the first hurdle cleared. Lovely woman, but I must be honest and say that she puts the fear of God into me.'

'I wonder why,' chuckled Cornelius, taking a moment to examine the pictures and certificates that were hanging on the walls (and secretly praying to himself that Robinson was going to be up to the task – the fellow was near-shaking with nervous excitement).

'Let's crack on, shall we?' huffed Robinson, skipping over to his desk and pulling open a drawer.

'What's the plan then, Doctor?'

'Well, as requested, I'll introduce you to some of the more *interesting* of my patients, give you the chance to have a little *chat* with them, then you can assess if anything seems out of the ordinary to you. I'll try and get hold of Gibbet too. Go easy on the little chap, wont you, Professor? He's not the most robust of fellows.'

Christopher Robinson pulled a collection of folders from the drawer and began to sort them into some sort of order.

'Any chance that you could arrange a meeting with Major Wolbury?' asked Cornelius, ambling over to the desk and spreading the files apart with the tip of his sausage-like finger.

Robinson looked a little worried, but nodded and muttered something about 'doing his best'.

'An' I need to be out of the grounds for lunch,' added Cornelius, stepping away from the desk, as Robinson thoughtfully selected three folders and tucked them under his arm. 'I'll be meeting up with Mr 'Ound,' he added as way of explanation.

'Perfect,' replied the young doctor, sweeping the hair out of his eyes with a gentle swish of his head. 'Gibbet is often sent on an errand to pick up sandwiches for the other orderlies; you can accompany him and see if he's got anything of interest to say on the matter. Come along, Professor, let me introduce you to the first of *our* patients. I think we'll begin with Captain Orwell.'

They walked along soulless corridor after soulless corridor, past more and more extremely "handy-looking" young orderlies (who patrolled said soulless corridors with expressions of dour-faced unfriendliness and the

42

demeanour of miffed mountain lions) until they came to a hallway with half a dozen steel doors on either side. A quartet of large, *resourceful-looking* chaps, all but bursting out of their white coats, got to their feet at Robinson and Lyon's approach. There was a slight ripple among the muscular wall of white fabric and through their midst pushed a stiff-necked little fellow with a salt-and-pepper beard, clutching a large clipboard to his chest.

'Ah, Dr Robinson!' he cried, self-importance quivering from every pore. 'A little late, but how very kind of you to actually show up at all!'

He stopped a few inches from Cornelius and craned his head upwards.

'And who is this, may I ask?' he sniffed, his nose twitching with affronted indignation.

'Professor Tinkle, may I introduce my assistant, Dr Coney?'

'Professor, is it? And you are here in what capacity, may I ask, sir?'

'Professor Tinkle was my teacher at Oxford. He's here, at my request, to offer his opinion – and may I just add that his opinion is one of world renown – on some of our more intriguing patients. If that's all right with you, that is, Dr Coney?' added Robinson, with barely-concealed sarcasm.

'I see. Well, how considerate of you to keep me up to date with everything, Dr Robinson. I do understand that I'm *only* your assistant, but I have been at this particular institution for a number of years now, and long before you were *gifted* the position. But then I haven't got friends in high places, have I, Dr Robinson? Well, Professor,' he continued, stepping back and offering Cornelius his hand, 'let me just say that it's an honour to meet you, sir. I do believe that I'm quite familiar with some of your papers, Professor Tinkle. Oh yes. Perhaps, if you have the time, we could discuss them, professional to professional, as it were, and,' he added, turning to look at Dr Robinson with a smug raising of an eyebrow, ' in private.'

'Cracking,' smiled Cornelius, pumping the jumpy little fellow's hand. 'Be delighted, Dr Coney.'

'Wonderful. And may I just add, Professor, how delightful it is to have someone of such high regard actually taking an interest in our work here. Well, I'd love to stop and chat all day, but things to do. The ward won't run itself, you know. Do drop by my office at any time, Professor Tinkle. Dr Robinson,' he nodded curtly, and then off he hopped, bustling with self-importance.

Christopher Robinson rolled his eyes and smiled apologetically. 'Sorry, Professor. The fellow's a frightful bore, but he's good at his job, and, believe it or not, I can't help but rather like the chap. He was angling for my position before I turned up. Bit of a sore point, as you might have guessed, but there you go, can't be helped. Come on. This way. Captain Orwell is expecting us.'

'Thank you, Small,' said Christopher Robinson, as one of the burly orderlies unlocked a steel door. Dr Robinson ushered Cornelius through the doorway, and the door was quickly, and very carefully, closed behind them.

The room (cell) that they had entered was spacious, very tidy, and furnished with a bed, a wash basin and a bookcase, along with a small table which was placed in the middle of the room. At that table sat a heavyset man with a head of thick grey hair, dressed in flannel pyjamas, and reading the morning's newspaper.

'Good morning, Ernest,' said Robinson, warmly.

'Good morning, Christopher Robinson,' replied the newspaper reader, glumly, without bothering to look up. 'If it is a good morning. Which I doubt.'

'Why, yes it is, Ernest. It is the very best of good mornings,' replied Robinson, chipperly. 'Ernest, you remember that I said I was bringing an old friend who'd like to talk with you? Well, here he is.'

'How marvellous. When's he going?'

'Professor Tinkle, may I introduce to you Captain Ernest Orwell, late of the 3rd (King's Own) Hussars.'

Captain Ernest Orwell, late of the 3rd (King's Own) Hussars, slowly lifted his head and held Cornelius' eye.

'Good morning, Captain,' said Cornelius, cheerfully.

'I'd rather you didn't,' huffed Orwell, gloomily.

'Didn't what?'

'Call me "Captain". It was such a terribly long time ago. To be honest, I'd rather forget about the war. Not that I'm complaining, you understand, but there it is.'

Dr Robinson smiled, pulled up a chair and sat down. He indicated that Cornelius should do the same. 'Mind if we join you?'

Orwell looked slowly from Robinson to Cornelius.

'Looks like you already have,' he said miserably. 'What is it that you want? Another of our little chats, Christopher Robinson? You must be bored by now. I know I am.'

Robinson chuckled. 'Not a bit of it, Ernest. I love hearing you talk, and you know it,' he grinned, sweeping the hair out of his eyes and oozing boyish charm. 'Come along, old fellow. Play the game. Just few minutes of your time and then you can return to your bloody newspaper, I promise. You never know, it might even be fun. What do you say?'

'Fun?' Orwell sighed. 'Fun. All right. Let's begin, shall we. Here we go gathering nuts in May, and all that. Let's enjoy ourselves. Why not?' He looked at Cornelius and held his enquiring gaze for near-on a full minute before speaking. 'They all died. There. Are you happy? Is that what you wanted to hear, Professor? I blew the bloody whistle and within minutes everybody under my command was dead.'

'But not you, Mr Orwell. You lived. You survived. An' not only did you survive, you managed to take out 'alf the bloody German army, if the reports are to be believed, that is. Like to tell me 'ow that 'appened?'

'Some live, some die. That's all there is to it. Did you serve, Tinkle?'

'I was with the Intelligence Corps,' smiled Cornelius. (Actually he was, along with The Hound, employed by *The Unseen League* as they battled against factions of the Nachzehrer Family [one of the twelve powerful vampire clans who hold dominion over much of the supernatural underworld] who had allied themselves with the German High Command during *The Great War*, but that was a longer conversation than Cornelius was prepared to [or saw the need to] get in to – so *Intelligence Corps* would do very nicely, thank you very much.)

'Were you, indeed? That sounds *very* nice. But then you've got brains, Professor. Anyone can see that.'

'Come along, Ernest. Don't be such a grouch. Be a good boy and answer the Professor's question.'

'If I must,' sniffed Orwell, giving Cornelius a dour once-over. 'Well, if you really want to know, Professor ... I can't remember.'

'Can't remember? What, not nothing?'

'Red. I remember red. And a terrible rage. There. There you have it. A *terrible red rage*. That's what I remember. Happy? Now, would you mind awfully if I get back to my morning paper? So much is happening in the outside world these days, I do like to keep *abreast* of it even if I can't be *a part* of it.'

'Tell the Professor about the horses, Ernest,' prompted Robinson.

''Orses?'

'Ah, yes. The horses. How could I forget? Thank you so much for reminding me, Christopher Robinson, I'd almost forgotten, but now I can remember and spend the rest of the day having bloody nightmares. How kind.'

'Have you ever heard a horse scream, Tinkle?' asked Orwell.

Cornelius nodded. 'I'm afraid I 'ave, son.'

'Really? More than most, I must say. Horsemen against bloody artillery. What were they thinking? Bloody idiots, the damned lot of them!'

'I won't argue with that, Mr Orwell, but what 'as screaming 'orses got to do with anything?'

'Ernest was discovered, covered in blood, amidst the mutilated bodies of a company of German soldiers,' interjected Robinson, 'all of them surrounded by a perfect circle of dead horses.'

'Was 'e indeed. Remarkable,' mused Cornelius. ''Ave you ever 'ad the thought, Mr Orwell, that you might 'ave experienced something of the supernatural?'

'*Supernatural*? [Hee-haw!] You're beginning to sound like little Gibbet.'

'I am?'

'Yes. He's always talking mumbo jumbo, is little Gibbet. You'd like him, Professor. Get along like a house on fire, I shouldn't wonder. Got no brains, has little Gibbet. Dr Coney has brains. Wolbury has brains. Even Christopher Robinson has brains (though sometimes I'm not sure he knows how to use them!) but the rest have got nothing but fluff between their ears, if you ask me. *Supernatural*! Tush! Stuff and nonsense, man! Now, really, gentlemen, if you've nothing better to do [hee-haw!] than to bother me with this flannel-waffling, I *have* got better things to do [hee haw!] with *my* day than discuss [hee-haw!] bloody [hee-haw!] fairy tales!'

'Come along, Professor, I think that we're upsetting the poor fellow. Ernest, I'll pop back and see you later this afternoon.'

'Most kind and thoughtful, Christopher Robinson. You'll see yourselves out, wont you? [Hee-haw] No, not at all, don't mention it.'

47

'Next up, Professor,' said Dr Robinson, plucking a folder from under his arm, 'is Baghinder Khan, a former Naik[6] in the 39th Garhwal Rifles.[7]'

'An' what's 'is story?' asked Cornelius, stroking his whiskers thoughtfully.

'Served on the Western Front. A one-man killing machine, by all accounts. Distinguished himself at The Defence of Festubert.[8] Delightful chap. Bit on the wild side, so brace yourself, Tinkle,' chuckled Robinson.

Small, the burliest of the burly orderlies, unlocked another of the steel doors. Christopher Robinson led Professor Cornelius Lyons/Isaiah Tinkle through the door and into a room (cell) near-identical to that of Captain Orwell's.

No sooner had the door locked shut behind them when an athletic-looking fellow with an enormous handlebar moustache (Cornelius liked him immediately) bounded towards them, snapped to attention and then, with a near-maniacal chortle, grabbed hold of Robinson's hand and pumped it vigorously.

'Hello, Baghinder,' chuckled Christopher Robinson. 'How are we today?'

'Oh, Dr Robinson,' beamed Baghinder Khan. 'Today I am most agreeable, yes I am. Today, you might say, I am full of ... *bounce*. Ha ha!'

''Ere, don't I know you?' sniffed Cornelius, as Baghinder Khan skipped over to him and enthusiastically shook his hand.

'Perhaps?' replied Khan, cautiously tilting his head to one side and sizing the old fellow up.

'Ain't you Sepoy[9] *"Tiger"* Khan, what fought for the British Empire Welterweight title against Johnny Summers[10] back in ... oo, when was it now ... 1912 ... or was it '13?'

Baghinder let go of Cornelius' hand, skipped backwards a couple of feet, and squinted quizzically at him.

'Why, yes! Yes, it was! I am that very same man who battled so very bravely against Johnny Summers. I would have been victorious too, if I hadn't have caught a dose of the flu a few days beforehand, let me tell you. Every hour afterwards I lived for my revenge, but then the blasted war came along and ruined everything!'

Baghinder started prowling around the room, energetically shadow-boxing.

'The fast left lead,' he growled. 'One, two, and maybe three. A feint, a slip to the fellow's right and then – BOOM! The overhand cross. Ah-ha! Like a tiger! Like a tiger. Like me. Sepoy "Tiger" Khan. Though I have had a promotion since then. Ha ha!'

Robinson looked at Cornelius, shrugged his shoulders and let go a boyish grin.

'Baghinder, it would be a great kindness if we could sit down and have a little chat with you for a moment. If it's no bother, that is?'

'Oh, no. No bother. No bother at all, Dr Robinson,' smiled Baghinder Khan, coming to a sudden halt and then all but leaping into one of the chairs that was placed around the table.

He sat looking at the two new arrivals, quivering with excitement.

'Well, come on! Take a seat! Take a seat and tell me what it is that I can do for you, gentlemen, on this most glorious of mornings?'

Robinson and Cornelius each took a chair opposite Khan.

'Baghinder, this is Professor Tinkle, he'd like to ask you a few questions.'

'Questions?' purred Khan, wiping his huge moustache with a cat-like sweep of the back of his hand. 'Ask away, my dear fellow. Ask away. Would you, perchance, like me to tell you about my glories in the boxing ring?'

'Another time, my friend.'

'Oh,' huffed "Tiger" Khan, looking a little crestfallen. 'Then what, may I ask, Professor Tinkle, would you like to know?'

'Since you've been an inma...patient at Five 'Undred Acre Asylum, 'as anything *untoward*, shall we say, 'appened 'ere?'

'*Untoward*? Whatever do you mean, Professor Tinkle?'

'I mean, for example, 'as anyone ever made mention of something, for example, called "The Achilles Project", for example?'

'Achilles? Project?' Baghinder Khan, stopped twitching and started looking perplexed. 'What is that?' he asked.

'Hhhhmmm,' hhhhmmmed Cornelius. 'Could I ask you, Baghinder, just 'ow it is that you come to find yourself 'ere at Five 'Undred Acre Asylum?'

Khan went very still. The only thing that moved were his eyes, which flickered back and forth between Dr Robinson and Cornelius. Cornelius couldn't help but notice that, all of a sudden, Baghinder's pupils seemed to have grown very large.

'Why do *you* think that I am here?' asked Khan, very quietly.

Cornelius shrugged. 'I was 'oping that you could tell me, my friend,' he smiled, suddenly noticing that there was a little chill in the air, and feeling the hairs on the back of his neck stand up on end.

Baghinder Khan looked slowly down at his hands, which he rested, palms up, on the table, his fingers slowly curling like an eagle's talons.

'It is very simple, my friend,' he purred, and his voice was as soft as silk. 'It is because ... AH HA! ...' he suddenly pounced forward towards Cornelius, sending his chair flying into the far wall with a loud crash, his arms outstretched, his fingers splayed, and roared 'I ... AM ... A ... TIGER!'

Both Cornelius and Dr Robinson were out of their seats in the flutter of a hummingbird's bottom, and frantically scuttling for the door, meeping like a pair of startled Salukis. However, mid-pounce Baghinder Khan veered away from them and started sprinting around the room and bouncing off the furniture, whilst swiping at imaginary foes with imaginary claws, and screeching 'I'M A TIGER! I'M A TIGER! I'M A TIGER! AH HA!' at the top of his voice.

'I think, Professor, that perhaps we should come back a little later, don't you?' smiled Dr Robinson, as he hastily banged on the door for Small to let them out.

Professor Isaiah Tinkle heartily agreed.

'I've saved the best till last,' beamed Dr Robinson, catching his breath and sweeping his fringe out of his eyes. 'Shouldn't really say this, but he's a bit of a favourite of mine. Well, with all of us, in fact. Isn't that right, Small?'

The burly Small, nodded his agreement, and probably broke Five Hundred Acre Asylum orderlies' union rules by breaking into a childlike grin.

'Is that so?' sniffed Cornelius, glancing back towards the closed door of Khan's cell with a look of barely-concealed alarm.

'The gentleman's name is Winston Lilicrap,' smiled Robinson, a playful twinkle sparkling in is eyes. 'The most decent sort you'll ever have the good fortune to meet. Apparently he was some sort of poet before the war. Not so good at it now, I'm afraid to say. He was at Ypres with the 1st Canadian Division. Took a terrible wound to the head at Gravenstafel Ridge.[11] The good Lord alone knows how he survived it. But survive it he did, and, according to his commanding officer, managed to decimate a couple of regiments of the German 4th Army in the process – single-handedly!'

Small led them to another steel door and began to unlock it.

Cornelius couldn't help but think to himself that he had somehow *slipped through the cracks* and was now picking his way through the very worst advent calendar in history.

'Come along, Professor,' smiled Robinson. 'We'll get this one done and then I'll try and find little Gibbet for you.'

Cornelius straightened his whiskers and then followed Dr Robinson through the door (which, he noted, Small didn't bother to lock after them).

Sitting at the table was a short, portly fellow with reddish blond hair and a happy countenance, seemingly absorbed in the act of getting the last smatterings from a honey-pot onto his last slice of toast.

'Hallo, Winston.'

'Oh, hallo, Dr Robinson,' smiled Winston Lilicrap, looking up from his task and returning a friendly little wave.

'I've brought a friend to see you. Hope you don't mind.'

'Not at all,' replied Lilicrap. 'Though it does appear that I've run out of honey, tiddly-tum-tum-tummy! Otherwise I'd offer you some for *your* toast. You did bring some, didn't you? Toast, I mean. I seem to have eaten all of mine.'

'That's awfully kind of you, Winston, old chap. But we've had breakfast already.'

Cornelius looked on stoically, whilst his stomach let out a sybaritic grumble.

'Winston, I'd like you to meet my dear friend, Professor Isaiah Tinkle.'

Winston Lilicrap looked up at Cornelius and smiled. 'Hallo,' he said. 'Do take a seat.'

Cornelius and Robinson sat down, while Lilicrap munched his way through the last slice of toast, all the while humming nonsensically to himself.

Suddenly the door was pushed open and Small stuck his head through the doorway.

'I've sent one of the lads off to see if we can find some more honey for Winston. I hope that's all right, Dr Robinson?'

'Thanks, Small. You're a brick,' said Robinson.

Small nodded at Robinson, then winked and smiled at Lilicrap, before turning away and gently closed the door behind him.

Winston Lilicrap continued humming contentedly to himself.

Dr Robinson coughed and egged Cornelius on with a little nod of his head.

'Mr Lilicrap,' began Cornelius.

'Yes?'

''Ow are you finding your stay 'ere at Five 'Undred Acres?'

'Oh, splendid. Everybody is *so* friendly. And I get lots of time to think about … *things*.'

'What sort of "things", Mr Lilicrap?'

'Well, let me see. Honey. Hums. Honey. Mostly honey. I do like honey. Do you like honey?' he asked, a sudden hint of hostility creeping into his voice.

Robinson subtly shook his head.

'Not much, truth be told, Mr Lilicrap. Not much at all.'

'Oh!' said Winston, trying to sound both sad and regretful.

'What 'appens 'ere at night, Winston? You don't mind if I call you Winston, do you, Mr Lilicrap?'

'Not at all, Professor … *Twinkle*?'

'Tinkle.'

'Tinkle. So sorry. And just what do you mean by "*at night*"?'

'Well, Winston, after Dr Robinson goes 'ome, what 'appens 'ere?'

Winston Lilicrap thought for a moment. And then he thought some more. Finally, when his thoughts were muddling around his head like hapless butterflies, he let out a long hum.

'Hhhhhhuuuummmmm? I don't seem to remember,' he said at last. 'Well, that's not strictly true. I *can* remember a few things, but just not in a way that makes any sense remembering them. So I don't. Or at least I try not to.'

Cornelius scratched his head.

'Do you think that you could try to remember, Winston?' smiled Dr Robinson. 'It might be very important.'

Winston Lilicrap rubbed his nose thoughtfully and stared at the empty honey pot.

'Well, sometimes, at night, Small and some of the other chaps wake me up and take me to see the Major and *his* friends.'

'Major Wolbury.'

'Yes! Do you know him?'

'I 'aven't 'ad the pleasure yet, Winston. But I'm 'oping to meet him later on today. So, tell me, what 'appens when you're with the Major an' 'is chums?'

'We play games,' said Winston. 'Though to be honest,' he whispered, leaning in closer and cupping a hand over his upper lip so as not to be overheard (though, as far as Cornelius could tell, there was no one around to overhear them), 'I don't really enjoy them very much.'

'What sort of games, Winston?' asked Dr Robinson, himself leaning in closer, and beginning to look a little concerned.

'Well,' began Lilicrap, quickly looking over his shoulder as if he was scared that someone might be listening, 'they all seem to revolve around trying to make me angry. But it doesn't work because I don't want to get angry. Which is funny, because the more I don't get angry, the more angry the Major seems to become. In fact, Major Wolbury gets very, very, very angry. But there you go. Some do and some don't, I suppose. Still, I don't know why he wants to make *me* angry because it seems a little bit unnecessary, if you want my opinion, because *he* becomes more than angry enough for all of us. Ho hum. Lot of silly bother, if you ask me. Tiddly-tum-tum-tee. Oh! Tea! Is it time for a little *something,* Christopher Robinson?'

Dr Robinson was about to answer, but what his answer was to be we'll never know (though Cornelius was very much hoping that the answer was going to be a "yes") because at that very moment the door opened and in walked the strangest little fellow that Professor Lyons had ever clapped eyes on (and believe me, due to his line of work, he'd clapped eyes on more than his fair share of strange little fellows).

The scrawny little chap couldn't have stood more than five feet tall, had a rosy pink complexion, piggy little eyes and a face like a punched potato.

'Ooh! Excuse me,' he whined in a high squeak. 'I haven't, have I? Ooh no, I haven't interrupted something important, have I? Ooh no!' he squeaked again, quivering with nerves.

'Not at all, Gibbet. Not at all,' said Dr Robinson, kindly.

'Ooh, that's a relief. I've just brought Winston some more honey,' he smiled anxiously, hoisting up a jar of honey for all to see.

'Oh-ho!' cried Lilicrap. 'HONEY!'

'Gibbet, this is Professor Tinkle, he's here to help me with my work. If it's no bother, would it be all right if the Professor accompanies you when you make your sandwich run to The Gallipot today?'

Gibbet looked at Cornelius with some alarm.

'Er … I … I … er … I suppose so,' he croaked, sounding thoroughly uncertain about the whole idea. 'Are you sure that you haven't got anything better to do, Professor? It really is quite boring. Collecting sandwiches and the like, that is.'

'I'd consider it a great kindness,' beamed Dr Robinson.

'A great kindness … right,' squeaked Gibbet, his voice wobbling in dismay. 'Ooh, before I forget, Dr Robinson; Major Wolbury has asked *me* to ask *you* if *you* would be so kind as to to go and see *him* in his office, right away. Apparently there have been some rather important developments that he'd like very much to talk over with you. He also asked me to tell you that he'd be most happy to talk to your guest as well. That'd be after lunch, now, I suppose.'

Gibbet squeezed out a nervous and toothless gurn.

'That's marvelous, thank you, Gibbet.'

'Not at all, Dr Robinson,' squealed Gibbet. 'Happy to help.' He looked over to Cornelius and tried very hard not to look like he might be quailing in any way whatsoever. 'Well then, Professor Tinkle. We'd better set off and get those sandwiches, or the lads will get upset. I'll just head off and get my basket and then I'll meet you by the front door in five minutes, give or take.'

He turned and looked at Lilicrap.

'Goodbye Winston. I'll pop by and see you later,' he said.

Winston Lilicrap, who's attention up until that point had been absorbed by the new pot of honey that Gibbet had just bought in for him, looked up and hummed in delight.

SEVEN
The Troublesome Tale Of Bertie Troynt

Dr Robinson and Cornelius offered their goodbyes to Winston Lilicrap and began the long walk through the maze of soulless corridors and towards the asylum's reception.

'Why do they call him Gibbet?' asked Cornelius.

Dr Robinson took a deep breath, held it for a stride or two, and then slowly let it out. 'Ah, the troublesome tale of Bertie Troynt,' he sighed. 'The story goes that poor old Bertie Troynt (formerly a Private in the 2nd West Riding Brigade) had the bad fortune to be discovered quivering, rather loudly by all accounts, under a barrel in a barn on the outskirts of the Ardre Valley by a reconnaissance party of Italian infantry at the beginning of the Battle of the Tardenois.[12] Every other member of his Section lay dead, in or around the barn. The captain of the Italians ordered Troynt to be shot on suspicion of cowardice, though Troynt pleaded that it wasn't the case. And oh, how poor Bertie Troynt pleaded for his life. So much so that the captain was so utterly disgusted by poor Bertie's sniveling display of self-preservation that he is reported as saying that he *"wouldn't waste a bullet on the mewling little runt"* (or words to that effect), and ordered for him to be hanged on the spot. And so, poor old Bertie was stood on his barrel and a noose was put around his neck, the rope thrown over and secured to the barn's stoutest beam. As the "bucket was kicked" from under him, so to speak, the rope snapped and Bertie Troynt tumbled to the ground physically unharmed (though God alone knows what the poor soul's mental state

57

must have been!). The captain, even more infuriated than before, ordered his men to repeat the process, which they did. But, before they could complete their grisly task, an attack by the German artillery struck the building and forced the Italians to flee, leaving poor old Bertie Troynt balancing on a barrel with a noose around his neck and the hellfire of the German mortars reigning down red murder among the flaming ruins of the barn.

'He was found by a party of 51st Highlanders, in pretty much the same state as he was left. Whatever "*crimes*" he may or may not have committed, the *powers that be* took mercy on him (praise the Lord!), obviously deciding that the poor little chap had suffered quite enough. And thus the name "Gibbet" was hung upon him, if you'll pardon the expression, from that day forth. Eventually he was shipped back home to Blighty, and here he's been, at Five Hundred Acre Asylum, ever since.'

'Jesus flippin' H Christ!' whistled Cornelius. 'I've 'eard some 'ard luck stories in my time, but that just about takes the flamin' biscuit. The poor little fellow, indeed.'

Robinson clicked his tongue and nodded his head in agreement. 'Ah! Here we are. Reception's through those doors there, Professor. I'm sure poor Bertie will be with you shortly. Go easy on the lad, won't you? I'd better run along and see what old Wol-Wol wants. I'll meet you back in my office after lunch. Will Mr Hound be with you?' he asked.

'Maybe, Dr Robinson, maybe. Let's see what I can get out of poor little Gibbet first, shall we?' sniffed Cornelius, unable to get the rather disturbing image of poor Bertie Troynt – standing on a flaming barrel with a rope around his neck and howitzer shells howling down all around him – out of his mind. 'Per'aps Mr 'Ound 'as a lead or two of 'is own to follow up on.'

It was a blustery day, and so Cornelius 'Dandy' Lyons and Bertie 'Gibbet' Troynt pulled up the collars of their jackets, pushed down their heads, and battled their way against the buffeting wind and along the path that led from Five Hundred Acre Woods to the village of Hartfield, where lay The Gallipot Inn and the asylum workforce's sandwiches.

'So, Bertie,' said Cornelius, ''ow long 'ave you been at the asylum for?'

'Since I got shipped back from the war, Professor Tinkle. They've been ever so kind to me, they have.'

'So you live there as well as work there? Is that right, Bertie?'

'That's right, Professor Tinkle. Why do you ask?'

'Well, I was just wondering if you could tell me about what 'appens there at night, after Dr Robinson an' 'is colleagues go 'ome for the evening?'

'I'm not sure that I know what you mean, Professor Tinkle.'

'Well, Bertie, are you aware of anything, shall we say, *out of the ordinary* that might be taking place in or around the asylum?'

'I just make the teas, Professor Tinkle. And sometime I go and collect the sandwiches for the lads,' replied Gibbet, nodding towards the empty wicker basket that he carried.

'So you don't know nothing about something called "The Achilles Project", then?'

Bertie Troynt sucked his lips and thought very hard for a moment.

'That's the thing that Major Wolbury is working on, isn't it?' he said at last.

'That's right, Bertie. Do you know anything about it?' asked Cornelius, kindly. 'Like what it's all about, for instance?'

'Sorry, Professor Tinkle, like I said, I just make the tea. "More tea, Gibbet," they say, and then I ask them if they'd like a biscuit with their tea, and sometimes they reply "that would be lovely, little Gibbet," and sometimes they say "no thank you, Gibbet", and I go and make them their tea, and then I bring them a biscuit or three, if they've asked for them, that is, or if they haven't, I don't.'

'An' you don't mind everybody calling you "Gibbet"?' asked Cornelius.

'I've been called a lot worse than that in my day, let me tell you, Professor Tinkle,' chortled Bertie Troynt. 'Er ... Professor, The Gallipot Inn is this way, not that way.'

Cornelius had turned from the path and was beginning to make his way towards Posingford Wood.

''Ere's where we part company for the moment, Bertie. I'm supposed to be meeting a friend for lunch,' he said, stopping and looking over his shoulder.

'Ooh!' squeaked Bertie, anxiously. 'A friend, you say? I do have to pick the sandwiches up for the lads, but I could come with you, for a little bit, if you'd like? I'm sure that no one would mind if I was a little bit late. Wouldn't even notice, I suspect. And it's nice to have someone to talk to. Makes a pleasant change, so it does.'

Cornelius looked down at the strange little fellow and couldn't help but smile.

'All right then, Bertie. Why not? Come an' say 'ello. An' then you best 'ead off an' pick up those sandwiches, or else, I reckon, there'll be all 'Ell to pay.'

Bertie Troynt smiled and all but danced a little jig of joy on the spot.

'Where are we going, Professor?' he asked.

'Posingford Wood, Bertie. Posingford Wood.'

'That's where the old shepherd's hut is, isn't it?'

Cornelius looked down at Bertie and raised an eyebrow.

'You know about that, do you?'

'Oh yes,' giggled Bertie. 'Everybody knows about the old shepherd's hut. It's the talk of the asylum, half the time. It's where Dr Christopher Robinson entertains his lady friends.'

Cornelius chortled to himself. 'Is it indeed, Bertie? Is it indeed. Well, good on Dr Christopher Robinson, aye?'

'It's also where they found them bodies, isn't it?' croaked Bertie, looking up at Cornelius with a querying and tragic look in his piggy little eyes. 'Posingford Wood, that is, not the old shepherd's hut. The poor souls.'

'So it is, Bertie. The poor souls indeed. What do you know about it? Any mention of it up at the asylum?'

Bertie Troynt shook his head sadly. 'I just make the teas, Professor Tinkle,' he said.

They picked their way through the wind-wobbled trees until they came into sight of the low and crumbling flint wall.

Cornelius began to whistle the opening bars of "*The Spaniard That Blighted My Life*".

Bertie Troynt clapped his hands together in merriment. 'Ooh! Ooh!' he cried. 'I know that song!' And then he began to sing in a high-pitched croak –

> "*List to me while I tell you*
> *Of the Span-iard that bligh-ted my life:*
> *List to me while I tell you*
> *Of the man who pinched my fu-ture wife.*"

Cornelius began to chuckle, and soon he found himself joining in with a hearty gusto, as the two of them clambered over the wall and made their way towards the sanctuary of the old shepherd's hut.

> "*'Twas at the bull fight where we met 'im*

We'd been watch-ing 'is dar-ing dis-play.
'Twas while I'd gone out for some nuts an'
a pro-gramme
The dir-ty dog stole 'er -away.
Oh, yes! Oh, yes!
But I've sworn that I'll 'ave my re-venge!"

Bertie lifted his piggy little nose to the sky and belted out
—

"He shall die! He shall die!
Tid-dly-i-ti-ti-ti-AAAAAAAAYYYYYYYIIIIIIII!"

Cornelius spun around and looked down at Bertie, for the last part of Bertie's rendition (the "AAAAAAAAYYYYYYYIIIIIIII!" bit) wasn't in the version that Cornelius knew. And to his great amazement he saw Bertie Troynt scampering his way back through the trees as fast as his little legs would carry him, squealing at the top of his voice – 'HELP! HELP! IT'S A WEREZLE!'

'Whatever is the matter, Bertie?' cried Cornelius, in astonishment.

But not for one second did little Bertie Troynt stop running.

'An' what, in the name of all the Gods an' their un'oly mothers, is a W*erezle*, when it's at 'ome?' sniffed Cornelius, scratching his head. Then he turned and saw The Hound (in canine form) gracefully trotting towards him, with what might have been a perplexed expression plastered over his wiry visage.

Cornelius looked back in the direction of Bertie Troynt's rapid retreat and couldn't help but chuckle.

EIGHT
The Gills Lap Mystery

'What, in the name of all *The Nine Realms*, is a *Werezle*?' asked The Hound, as he cut the last of Miss Sand's delicious steak and ale pies into quarters and passed a slice to Cornelius.

'I think *you* are, 'Aitch,' chortled Cornelius.

'And what, in the name of Cerberus's chew toy, was that?' snorted the were-hound, flicking a wiry and reddish ear (faintly covered with white spots) in the direction of the hut's door.

'*That*,' answered Dandy, between meaty munches, 'is what is known as a Bertie Troynt.'

'Bertie Troynt? Dr Robinson's orderly chappie? Gibbet, wasn't it?'

'That's the fellow. Nervous little tyke,' cackled Cornelius, wiping pie-juice from his Newgate Knocker with the tips of his fingers. 'Though, 'aving 'eard 'is sorrowful tale, I can't say that it's any wonder.'

The Hound eyed the slice of pie in his hand and took a moment to savour the wonderful cocktail of aromas wafting towards his bulbous black hooter.

'So, Dandy,' he began, taking a large, loud chomp, 'what did you discover at the asylum?'

Cornelius took a moment to swallow his mouthful before answering.

'I met with three of Robinson's patients.'

'And?'

'Mad as a bag o' badgers in a Billings'urst barn, the 'ole sorry lot of 'em. Poor sods. 'Owever, if we were to follow along the path of thought that suggests it were a were-

63

beast, of some variety, what plucked the noggins from those poor unfortunates in Posingford Wood, then I'd put me thrupp-nee bit on one Mr Baghinder Khan, late of the 39th Garhwal Rifles,' he mused.

'Indeed?' enquired The Hound, raising an interested eyebrow as he passed Cornelius the third quarter of pie and then picked up the last piece for himself. 'And what is it that arouses your suspicions about Mr Baghinder Khan, late of the 39th Garhwal Rifles, old chap?'

'Well, 'Aitch, Mr Baghinder Khan, late of the 39th Garhwal Rifles, thinks 'e's a tiger. Almost scared the living shit out of me, let me tell you. 'Owever, let's just suppose, for one minute, that Mr Baghinder Khan actually is some sort of were-tiger, or per'aps some other sort of supernatural *Pantherra tigris* killing ma–'

'*Pantherra tigris tigris*,' interjected The Hound. 'If we assume that Mr Baghinder Khan is a were-tiger of Bengali origins, that is.'

'I stand corrected – *Pantherra tigris tigris* (thank you very much, 'Aitch – for fuck's sake!) killing-machine. Might it be that 'e gets let out on the night of the full moon so as those 'oo run *The Achilles Project* can see just what 'e can do? Imagine a regiment made up of were-tiger soldiers coming at you!' he shuddered, licking his lips before devouring his delicious piece of pie.

The Hound swallowed his own last mouthful, thoughtfully licked clean his claws and looked dolefully down towards the empty plate.

'I have a different theory,' he said at last.

Cornelius wiped his facial furniture with a handkerchief, and looked up.

'Well go on then, 'Aitch. What 'ave you got?'

'I spent the morning scouting around Posingford Wood, where the murder victims bodies were found, and then moved on to Gills Lap, where their heads were discovered.'

'An'?'

'Gills Lap is indeed an enchanted spot. As our dear friend Pook Alberich Albi[13] might say – a *place of power*.'

'Druidic?'

'Undoubtedly. And perhaps far older. But be that as it may, I made a rather unsettling discovery whilst digging around up there.'

'Did you? Well, go on then, 'Aitch, what did you find?'

The were-hound held Cornelius' gaze and an excited sparkle glinted in his walnut-coloured, almond-shaped eyes.

'Skulls,' he growled.

'Skulls!' gasped Cornelius. 'What, are you telling me that you found more 'uman 'eads?' he spluttered, unable to mask his dismay.

'Not human heads, my friend, but the skulls of all manner of creatures: mouse, rat, rabbit, adder, weasel, cat, fox, badger, deer, sheep, even, I'm most sorry to have to say, dog (collies by the looks of them, God rest their souls).'

'Well,' sniffed Cornelius, 'we are in the middle of the countryside, old fellow. You'd expect to find a lot of animal remains in a place like that.'

'Let me expand further, my dear friend. You are quite correct, Cornelius, one *would* expect to find the skeletal remains of all manner of British wildlife, that is true, but I could find nothing, I repeat, *nothing*, but skulls!'

'Now that is weird,' rasped Cornelius.

'Not only that, but all the skulls had been buried in pairs – two mouse skulls, two rat skulls, two rabbit skulls, two adder skulls, et cetera, et cetera, et cetera. On closer examination I'd say that the first pair (the mice) had been dispatched and buried a little over a year ago, and that each successive killing, each double murder, had been committed about four weeks apart, give or take a few days here and there.'

'From full moon to full moon, per'aps!' snarled Cornelius.

'Precisely!' growled The Hound.

'So what do you think that we're looking at 'ere, 'Aitch? Might it just be that you 'it the nail squarely on the 'ead with your original 'unch, when you suspected that it might be some sort of ghastly occult ritual?'

'It would seem the most likely explanation,' sighed the were-wolf-wolfhound, regretfully shaking his massive and tousled head. 'But something bothers me about the whole shebang. Why progress, full moon by full moon, from the killing of mice and rats to the killing of dogs and men?'

'Maybe they've been building up to something big an' 'ad to get the 'ang of it first (the ritual, that is, or whatever "it" is)?' suggested Cornelius. ''Ere, do you think that we should knock Five 'Undred Acre Asylum on the 'ead? This 'ole *Achilles Project* looks like it might be nothing but a bit of a red 'erring,' he added hopefully; for, the truth be told, the thought of returning to the asylum wasn't one that he held with much joy. The place gave him the heebie-jeebies.

The Hound thought for a moment.

'No,' he said at last. 'No. Best keep ourselves open to all possibilities until we know for certain, old chap. Go back and see Dr Robinson and inform him of our suspicions. Then telephone Captain Milner and see if he can get us any back-up from *The Unseen League*. For this night will bring the full moon,' he snarled, a sly grin playing on his thin black lips, 'and, as She rises, so will we capture these contemptible scoundrels and thus bring an end to their nefarious affairs forever!'

''Ear, 'ear!' cried Cornelius.

NINE
A Most Peculiar Brew

'Major Wolbury is waiting for you in his office, Professor Tinkle,' smiled the horse-faced Nurse Rooney, as Cornelius entered the Five Hundred Acre Wood Asylum and shook the wind from his whiskers.

'Perfect,' smiled Cornelius, thinking to himself that this would save him some time and that he could get out of this infernal place all the sooner, as he turned down the collar of his jacket and straightened his tie.

'If you'll just step this way, Professor, I'll take you right there.'

Nurse Rooney knocked on the closed door of Wolbury's office.

There was a short pause before a high and breathy voice barked 'Come!'.

The horse-faced colonial smiled at Cornelius and opened the door. Cornelius couldn't help but notice that her smile didn't quite reach her eyes. *Though to be fair*, he thought to himself, as he returned a buttery gurn of his own and walked past her as she held the door open for him, *it did have an 'eck of a long way to travel!*

Major Wolbury looked up from the papers he had been studying and peered over the rim of his spectacles in the new arrival's direction.

'Ah, Professor Tinkle, I presume?' he said, rising from the table and striding over to take Cornelius' hand.

'Indeed it is, sir,' beamed Cornelius/Tinkle. 'A great pleasure to finally meet you at last, Major. I've 'eard so much about you.'

Major Wolbury let out a little hoot of delight.

'If you had not said it first, I would have said the very same,' he grinned. 'Dr Robinson has spoken so very highly of you. Please, take a seat. Could I offer you some tea, Professor?"

'That would be cracking.'

'Excellent. Nurse Rooney, some tea, if you please.'

'Right away, Major,' replied Nurse Rooney, turning on her heels and closing the office door behind her.

Wolbury sat down behind his desk and scrutinised his visitor.

Cornelius took the opportunity to do the very same.

Major Wolbury was a middle-sized man in his fifties. His body was square and his arms were long. He had an unruly mop of downy grey hair, a little beak-like nose, and large, piercing brown eyes under a pair of large, horn-rimmed round spectacles.

'How did you enjoy your morning at Five Hundred Acre Asylum, Professor?' asked Wolbury, taking off his spectacles and polishing them on the cuff of his jacket.

'Most remarkable,' replied Cornelius.

'Most remarkable indeed, Professor. Dr Robinson has done such sterling work with these extraordinary fellows. Five Hundred Acre Asylum has become the last sanctuary for these poor men. As you have no doubt learned, Professor Tinkle, all of these fellows excelled in The War; perhaps a little too much, some might say, which is why they find themselves here. This institution,' he sighed, replacing his glasses and lancing Cornelius with a strigine stare, 'is the only thing that has kept them from the hands of the hangman and the firing squad. In the *field of blood*, Professor, each of them was considered a hero. However, their insatiable blood-lust, their (and, alas, there is no other word for it) *genius* for murder – which made them invaluable and so highly praised and valued in the arena of war – in times of peace is, quite frankly, unacceptable. For

68

they are murderers, Professor! Killers, to a man. So, how should the society that so profited from their abilities in times of need now act when that particular ... *talent* ... is no longer required? When peace returns most men can *switch off* their desire to harm their fellow man. Some, it seems, cannot. Perhaps they were never *normal* men at all. Perhaps they have been murderers all of their lives and The War simply released the demons that lay within. Who can say? But it is undeniable that those *demons*, once awoken, are now most reluctant, to say the very least, to lie back down again.

'Our work here is to help these men, to treat them with the respect that their wartime heroics deserve, to repay the debt that our country owes them but – Ah, Nurse Rooney. Tea. Most marvellous.'

'Shall I pour, Major?' asked Nurse Rooney, setting down a tray brimming with tea-making paraphernalia.

'Most excellent. Please do, Nurse Rooney. Milk and sugar, Professor?'

'Just milk, please. Ta very much.'

Nurse Rooney poured two cups of tea and handed a cup and saucer to Cornelius with a long-faced smile.

'That will be all, Nurse Rooney,' said Wolbury, lifting his cup and saucer to his beak-like hooter and taking a deep and satisfied sniff.

'A most peculiar brew,' he said, peering over the steamed-up lenses of his spectacles. 'I first became acquainted with it during my time in Hong Kong. I prefer for mine to be a little cooler,' he smiled, placing the cup and saucer back on the desktop. 'Sensitive palate,' he added.

Cornelius took a doubtful sniff of his own teacup, and was met with a most unusual aroma. *What*, he wondered with dismay, *was this newfangled fashion for exotic teas?*

'Please,' said Wolbury, pointing a finger at Cornelius' cup. 'I hope you enjoy it.'

Cornelius took a tentative sip – and was delighted to discover that the tea was rather delicious. Huzzah!

'Very nice indeed, Major,' he smiled, taking a longer swig. 'I could get used to that.'

Wolbury let out a hoot of delectation.

'Now then, Major, I was wondering if you could tell me anything about something called "The Achilles Project"?' asked Cornelius, draining his cup and returning it and its companion saucer to the Major's desk. If truth be told, he was already getting a little bit bored of being in the asylum, and so decided that there was no point beating about the bush and that he might as well get straight down to matters, for though he wanted to find out more about the mysterious *Achilles Project*, he'd much prefer to be out of here and helping The Hound pursue his unsettling discoveries regarding Gills Lap.

Wolbury held his enquiring gaze for a long moment, and then checked the time on his wristwatch.

Cornelius couldn't help but notice that it must have been a lot colder than he thought outside, for, all of a sudden, his fingertips were beginning to tingle.

'You're not Professor Tinkle, are you?' huffed Wolbury, his eyes seemingly growing larger and larger behind the lenses of his spectacles. 'Who sent you? The police? MI7? *The Unseen League*? I thought that the young fool Robinson was growing suspicious. Not that it matters.'

Cornelius tried to reply but found, to his absolute horror, that he didn't seem to be able to speak. And, what's more, he was rooted to his chair like a marble statue. The tea! It must have been drugged! What a damned fool he was to have let his guard down like that! And now here he was, frozen like a paralysed pheasant in a bird feed factory, unable to move a muscle to defend himself against this arch-villain!

Wolbury dropped his head beneath his heaving shoulders and seemed to be laughing into his chest (like the evil madman that he undoubtedly was). But, as he swiped his glasses from his face and looked up again, Cornelius was astounded to see that the man was positively weeping.

The Major stood up from his desk, walked towards Cornelius and placed a hand gently on his shoulder.

I'm so sorry,' he sobbed, a look of disgusted horror on his tear-stained visage. 'He makes me do it. You don't know what he's like. He's so –'

Cornelius heard the door open.

'Leave us!' hissed a voice.

Wolbury dropped his head to his chest like a first year fag being told to *make himself scarce* by the school bully, and fled.

The door snapped quietly shut behind him.

TEN
The Moonlight Reveals Us

With mounting terror, Cornelius listened to the sound of the slow footfall approaching him. He tried to move, but his muscles were frozen rigid. He tried to speak, but his tongue was like a lead weight in his mouth. Was this how it ended? After all these years? Cornelius '*Dandy*' Lyons – one-time pride of the Regency Prize Ring, the darling of The Fancy[14], a (former) prince of Fairyland, one half of one of (if not *the*) most internationally renowned paranormal investigation agencies (*Lyons & Hound* – established 1895) in the world today – murdered by some horrible fiend? His bewhiskered old noodle plucked from his shapely shoulders like a cork from a bottle of chilled brown beer? If he could have, Cornelius Lyons would have wept.

The footsteps shuffled to a halt behind him, and Cornelius felt hot breath against the back of his neck.

'So much blood,' sighed the voice, in a breathy, high squeak. 'So much blood.'

And even before the terrifying new arrival stepped around and stood before him, Cornelius knew who it was.

Bertie Troynt? he thought, in amazement. *Little Gibbet!*

'It seeped through the mud of the trenches,' whispered little Bertie Troynt, looking fiercely into Cornelius' eyes. And if he could have, Cornelius would have quailed as the black pits of abhorrence that were Bertie's piggy little peepers pierced him to the very core of his dapper, and decidedly decent, soul. 'Down it seeped, from the mutilated corpses of men, from the murdered bodies of boys, and deep into the earth. Down and down, deeper and deeper, until it reached where I lay; forgotten for so long. So many ages. Abandoned. Disregarded. Dishonoured. It was the blood that awakened me. It was the blood that brought me back. So much blood. I never thought it possible. Up and up I reached, with the little strength that had returned to me. It was the blood that nourished me, fed me, called me. So much blood, so much death, so much ... *sacrifice*. It was like the old days, my days of glory, when my children would send me the trophies they had taken from their enemies. "Bring me their heads," I asked of them. And they did.

'Rising upwards like a feeble shoot awakening from the darkest winter, I followed the scent of death. Upwards and upwards! Rising through the mud, through the disfigured remains of men – who lay scattered, betrayed by their kings, and sent to their deaths like tethered lambs – and into the daylight once more! Free I was! Born again!'

Bertie Troynt suddenly pulled his terrifying stare from Cornelius and turned and walked, hands held behind him, towards the desk.

'And the only living thing that I found, the only vessel that remained, was this snivelling little creature!' he croaked, sinking his head between his narrow shoulders with a disgusted huff. 'This pathetic little weakling. This runt. But, bit by bit, little by little, I have grown stronger. In time, my powers will return; head by head, stronger and stronger I grow. Strongest of all when the moonlight reveals us for what we are. Oh yes!' cried Gibbet, spinning back around and grinning, a ghastly and ghoulish gurn engraved upon his punched-potato-like kisser, 'I am not alone! For this war of yours, this *Great War (ha ha!)*, aroused others like me from their slumber deep beneath the land of heroes, the land of the Gauls. And I will find them all, and teach them, and tend and nurture them back to health, until our powers are replenished and the world worships us once more.

'Know me and fear me, foolish mortal!' he laughed, with a squeal-like piggy roar, pumping his skinny fist into the sky. 'For I am *Camulos*[15] – the boar king! War god of the Remi![16] And I have returned to sow sorrow to the world of men!'

ELEVEN
Gibbet & Lilicrap Meet A Werezle

The wind playfully knocked the treetops together, making a susurrous chorus of whispers that chased away the timorous clouds and so revealed a full moon that peered across the inky darkness of the night with an unblinking gaze of eternity.

Through the rattling trees of Posingford Wood, little Gibbet and Winston Lilicrap stumped merrily along; Lilicrap humming happily to himself and tugging a sturdy length of rope behind him. Attached to the end of Winston's sturdy length of rope were the stumbling figures of two unfortunate souls, each bound at the wrists and each with a cloth sack over their head. Both of them, drugged as they were (one encased in tweed and built like an orangutang raised on a diet of whisked eggs, fresh oysters and organic porter; the other, tall and slender, and of a rather boyish bearing), slipped and staggered with a dreary gait, as if slowly and uncertainly awakening from a nightmare-filled slumber.

'Are we going to play *the game*, Bertie?' asked Lilicrap, breaking off from his cheery little hum to address his companion.

'How many more times!' squealed his diminutive chum, all but stamping his foot in irritation. 'Don't call me that! Not when we're out and about and the full moon has come back over the forest. My name is *Camulos*!'

'Sorry,' said Winston, wrinkling his nose thoughtfully. 'And ... what was my name again?'

Gibbet sighed his annoyance and waved his tiny fists in the air in frustration. '*Artaius*!' he snapped. 'Your name is

Artaius. The great war god of the Nervii![17] Please, do try and remember, it's very important. *You* are Artaius[18] – the mighty Bear God.'

Winston Lilicrap/Artaius, the mighty Bear God, scratched his ear (in a nice sort of way) with his free hand and thought some more.

'But I'm a man,' he said. 'Aren't I? At least I was the last time I looked.'

'Then look again,' snorted Camulos/Bertie Troynt. 'For the moonlight reveals us for what we *really* are. See?'

'Oh! I do see! Yes. Yes that is a bit like a bear, I suppose,' said Artaius, peeking down with some surprise at his bearlike feet and then examining the long, lethal-looking claws on his fingers as they glistened like instruments of death in the moonlight.

He looked over at his dear friend, Bertie ... no ... Camulos ... and was rather bemused to see that although Bertie/Camulos still retained his small and somewhat puny physique, he did seem to have grown little tusks that jutted from his lower lip, and that his shoulders hunched over more than was usual, and that he had sprouted a stiff crest of thick hair that ran from the top of his potato-like head all the way down his scrawny neck and disappeared under the collar of his stripy pullover.

'Bother!' said Winston/Artaius, 'Now that *is* a very funny thing indeed. It's not easy not having much brain, Camulos,' he said, reaching over and scratching his other ear. 'Dr Coney said I'd left most of it in Ypres, that's in *Bell-jam*, in case you were wondering. Perhaps, when we've finished here, we could go and look for it.'

'In time, Artaius. In time. But first we must grow stronger.'

'Stronger? But I feel very strong indeed. In fact, I feel stronger than I've ever felt before.'

'That's good,' smiled Camulos. 'That's good. But you were stronger once. Much stronger. And so was I. Come on,

Artaius, let's get to the bridge and then you can pull their heads off. And then we can play that game that you like so well. And we'll drop their bodies into the river, and we can see whose comes out on the other side first. It's my turn to choose, if you remember rightly, so I'm going to pick the big fellow with the silly moustache.'

'But I was going to choose him!' sniffed Artaius, sadly. 'Are you sure that it's your turn to pick first? I can't remember.'

'Yes, it is,' said Camulos rather quickly (which made Artaius suspect that perhaps Camulos was lying, but he couldn't be sure). 'Now let's hurry along because earlier today I saw a Werezle,'

'A *Werezle*!' cried Artaius, with some alarm. 'What's a *Werezle*?'

'A *Werezle* is one of the fiercer animals,' said Camulos, looking about in a worried fashion.

Artaius followed Camulos' troubled gaze. 'But *what*, exactly, is it?'

'A creature of hostile intent, that's what it is.'

'Then I think,' suggested Artaius, 'that we'd better hurry along to the bridge. Just in case we run into it ... the Werezle, that is, not the bridge.'

'That's what I've been saying. Now come along, let's play our little game and then we can head up to Gills Lap and have a little *something*.'

'Honey?' beamed Artaius, humming with excitement.

'No, not honey, you silly old bear. Heads! It is heads what make us stronger, not honey. Like in the old days.'

'Oh. Sorry. I forgot.'

As they reached the bridge the bright, all-seeing moon hung high in the sky above them.

'Take their hoods off, Artaius,' said Camulos, 'and we will begin.'

With a swipe of his claws, Artaius ripped open Cornelius' bonds and then plucked the hood from his head.

Even though the drugs were beginning to wear off, Cornelius' brain still felt fuzzy, his vision was blurred, and his limbs felt like treacle. He shook his head to try and clear the fuzziness, and, despite his best efforts, slowly fell over.

Camulos danced a little jig of joy, his trotter-like feet clattering against the wooden bridge most musically as he began to sing –

"He shall die! He shall die!
Tiddly-i-ti-ti-ti-ti-ti-ti!"

As Camulos danced and sang, Artaius pulled the hood from the second of their prisoners. With a cry of alarm, he leapt back, putting both of his murderous paws to his snout in horror.

'Whatever is the matter, now?' huffed Camulos, halting mid jig.

'That's Christopher Robinson!' cried Artaius, in some confusion, pointing with a knife-like digit in the direction of Christopher Robinson, as the young doctor swooned to the floor with a breathless gasp.

'What of it? We need his head more than he does.'

'But he's my friend.'

'You have to do it, Artaius. I would do it for you but I haven't got the strength. But you have, and so do it you must, otherwise we'll stay like this forever, and then who in their right friggin' mind is going to bow down and worship us?'

'But ...'

'DO IT!' roared Camulos, the Boar God.

'But ...'

'DO IT!' squealed the ancient war god of the Remi. 'He must die!' he bellowed, shaking his skinny fists to the

78

moon-lit sky. 'He must die! Tiddly-i-ti-ti-ti-ti-ti-AAAAAYYYYYIIIIIIIIII!!!!!' he squawked.

Artaius swung his head round to see what Camulos was AAAAAYYYYYIIIIIIIIII!!!!!ing about, and was rather concerned to see his dear friend Bertie Troynt/Camulos, mighty war god of the Remi, fleeing across the bridge as fast as his piggy little legs would carry him.

Artaius swung his head back round – and got the shock of his life. For leaping towards him was what could only be described as a *Werezle*! Seven-and-a-half feet tall, covered in wiry golden hair, the head of a monstrous dog and the body of a champion middleweight boxer, with (possibly) a murderous grin (it was hard to say) warped along its thin black lips, jaws like a bear-trap, teeth like poniards, talons like scythes, a look of demented hunger glistening in its almond-shaped and walnut-coloured eyes, and dressed in what appeared to be an enormous pair of plus fours of the most exquisite shade of scarlet.

The beast landed two feet in front of the startled Artaius.

'Frightfully sorry,' said the Werezle, apologetically, 'You do seem like an awfully decent sort, old chap, but under the circumstances it seems best not to take any chances. I'm sure you understand.'

And, like a bolt of lightening, a murderous overhand right exploded onto the ursine-like jaw of Winston Lilicrap/Artaius, great bear god of the Nervii, sending him sprawling unconscious to the floor with an almighty thump.

The Hound quickly bound the strange little man-bear with a length of rope that happened to be on the floor of the bridge, and then dashed to Cornelius' side.

'Hello, old chap, been getting yourself into all manner of mischief, I see. I turn my back for one minute ...' he tutted with kindly concern, gently helping his whiskery chum to his feet. 'How are you feeling, old flower?'

Cornelius shook his head and rubbed the back of his neck.

'All the better for seeing you, 'Aitch, I'll tell you that for nothing,' he rumbled, blinking heavily and trying to regain his focus.

'Stay here with Dr Robinson till I get back, there's a good fellow,' smiled the were-hound, with a good-natured wink, as he gently replaced the cloth bag back over the head of the prostate form of Dr Christopher Robinson. 'I'm going on a little pig hunt.'

TWELVE
An Unexpected Horror

Cornelius Lyons lent against the metal railings and took a moment to enjoy the bracing sea-breeze, as it playfully ruffled his whiskers and almost blew the hat from his head. From the beach below, a gang of seagulls peeled themselves into the sky and loudly rushed to meet a small fishing boat that was returning to the shore. He followed their effortless flight for a moment and then turned his attention to the weekend crowd sauntering along Brighton's seaside promenade below him, decked, for all the world to see, in their Sunday finery (most of them probably having travelled down from *The Old Smoke*[19] for the day to take in the sea air), and he chuckled to himself as he recalled the words of his old pal, Whelk-faced Willie the Wheeze (the lisping landlord of *The Concealed Arms*), who had once noted that – "when a man ith tired of London, Dandy, he'th probably grown up a little bit".[20] And Cornelius Lyons couldn't help but think to himself that it was good to be back home again.

Slowly he turned his back to the wind, put a steadying hand on his coachman's bowler, and looked down at the giant hound sitting patiently at his side.

'Best we 'ead back 'ome, Jeffries, my dear old friend,' he said to the massive wolfhound. ''Is Nibbs will be waiting for us.'

Jeffries tore his nose from the wind, looked up at the old duffer with eyes that held the wisdom of a thousand lives, and smiled (as only a wiry sighthound can when being buffeted by a brisk breeze on a blustery day).

As they entered through the door of One Punch Cottage, Missus Dobbs was coming down the stairs with an overcoat folded over one arm and a matching trilby hat tucked under the other.

'Oh, hello, Ducky,' she gurned. 'Mr Hound is waiting for you. That lovely Captain Milner has just arrived. Shall I bring you all up a nice cup of tea?'

'Smashing, Missus Dobbs,' smiled Cornelius. 'That'd be lovely.'

'So,' said Milner, looking about The Study at the piles of unpacked boxes and the small mountains of books that lay scattered around the room, 'how are you settling into your new home?'

'I think we'll be most happy here, thank you, Captain,' replied The Hound. 'Don't you, Dandy?'

''Ell yes! Blessing to 'ave found it, truth be told. Property being 'ow it is these days,' said Cornelius, playfully scratching behind Jeffries' ear, and making the wolfhound's mighty rear leg thump furiously against the floor.

'So, please tell us, Captain Milner, what's the news from Five Hundred Acre Asylum?'

Milner leant back in his chair and whistled.

'Well,' he began, 'where to begin?'

''Ow's Dr Robinson doing?'

'Oh, Chris is fine. A little shaken up, but nothing he won't get over. Made of sturdy stuff is Christopher Robinson, let me tell you. In fact, he's been offered a new job. Due to the sterling work he's been doing with the chaps at Five Hundred Acre Asylum, *The League* has headhunted him and asked him to join the staff at The Mound.[21] I'm delighted to say that Chris has agreed. Capital choice all around, if you ask me.'

'An' what of 'is old patients?' asked Cornelius. 'Lilicrap an' Khan an' Orwell, an' the rest of the poor sods that I didn't 'ave the privilege to encounter? An' what about poor old Bertie Troynt?'

'All heading to The Mound with Chris,' smiled Milner. 'Safest place for them, I'd say, now that Five Hundred Acre Asylum is being closed down, thank God.' He shook his head and stamped the tip of his walking stick gently against the floor. 'The most extraordinary affair, imaginable.'

'A most extraordinary affair indeed,' concurred The Hound, thoughtfully tapping his snout with the tips of his dirk-like talons. 'If their subsequent interviews are to be believed, Troynt, Lilicrap and Orwell were all possessed by the spirits of long-forgotten Celtic war deities, awoken from their long years of neglect by the mass murder of millions of young men on sacred Gallic tribal territories. Remarkable! Though, in retrospect of the horrors and absolute mindless insanity of that particular conflict, perhaps not completely implausible.'

Milner shook his head again.

'As you know all too well, Professor, it would seem that Troynt was possessed by *Camulos* the boar, war god of the Remi, Lilicrap by *Artauis* the bear, war god of the Nervii, and Captain Orwell by *Rudiobus*[22], the horse god of Carnutes.[23] There's a lifetime's worth of work in studying those poor blighters, let me tell you.'

'An' what about Baghinder Khan?' enquired Cornelius. 'Was 'e a Gallic god of war or is 'e actually a tiger, of some sort or another??'

'Not one hundred percent certain, as yet, Professor. Still under observation, from what I'm told.'

'And Major Wolbury?' asked The Hound.

'Relieved of his post and under investigation. Though the word on the street is that the poor fellow has had a complete breakdown. It would appear that the Major had utterly fallen under the spell of Troynt/Camulos. Hard to say what will happen to him, should he ever recover, but I don't doubt that his high-flying friends will see him right should any charges be pressed. But whatever happens, his career is finished.'

'An' *The Achilles Project*?[24] Did you manage to discover what that was all about?'

Milner rubbed his temples with his fingertips. 'Not really,' he sighed. 'It seems that there was some suspicion of supernatural occurrences surrounding all of the patients at Five Hundred Acre Asylum, the military got wind of it and wanted to see if there was any way that their boffins might be able to isolate what made these poor fellows such extraordinary killing machines. One has to wonder why on earth they haven't had their fill of warfare, the bloodthirsty fools? If that last war isn't *the war to end all wars,* then God help us all, though why the hell He should bother, I suppose, is beyond me!' he snorted.

At that moment Missus Dobbs entered The Study staggering under a tray on which balanced all the tea-making equipment and paraphernalia that one could possibly imagine, along with half a ton of assorted biscuits.

'Ooh, cracking!' cackled Cornelius, leaping to his feet to help the little House-Fairy with the tray, Jeffries following fast on his heels.

'Could I be a nuisance and enquire where the *conveniences* are?' asked Milner.

'Follow me, Ducks, and I'll show you the way,' gurned Missus Dobbs, holding the door open for him, and looking absolutely delighted with herself as she cast a gloriously self-congratulatory glance in the direction of the teapot.

As Captain Milner carefully made his way back down the stairs (stairs were not on his list of favourite things!) towards The Study, he overheard Mr Hound and Professor Lyons engaged in a most peculiar conversation. Being, in part, a polite young fellow and also, by profession, an agent of a top-secret organisation, he found himself eavesdropping by The Study door.

'You first, old stick,' said the low, clipped tones of the were-hound.

'Oh, no, 'Aitch, I wouldn't 'ear of it. After you, I insist,' came the reply.

'But you are such the connoisseur, my dear fellow. You know how much I value your opinion on matters like these.'

'Like I said, 'Aitch, I'm sure that you'll understand, but, what with recent events, I seem to find myself being a little more 'estitant than is my normal wont.'

There was a long pause followed by a stoic sniff.

'What if we do it ... *together*?'

'Hhhhmmm. All right. I suppose so.'

'Right. Good man. That's the ticket. On the count of three, then. Ready? One, two ... three ...'

To Milner's dismay, there was a short pause followed by a chorus of stifled cries of agony and what sounded like the smash of crockery, all accompanied by the frantic and deep barking of Jeffries.

He burst through the door, dropping his walking stick and heaving the Webley Mark VI revolver from his shoulder holster ... and was met with the most thoroughly perplexing sight.

Writhing on the floor, his hands clutched to his throat as if he were being attacked by an invisible king cobra, rolled Professor Lyons, gasping and gagging most alarmingly, while beside him The Hound was clawing his way painfully along the floor towards the door, one hand stretched out before him in an imploring gesture that silently screamed "HELP ME!", his back arched and his terrifying jaws spread wide apart as he dry-retched and made horrendous hacking noises. Jeffries, the giant wolfhound, leapt between them, barking excitedly and furiously wagging his great tail.

Around them lay the shattered remains of two teacups.

NOTES

1. *Wodin-Poke*
A magical spell cast upon the *uninitiated* to give them the short-term ability to see through enchantments of misdirection, masking and concealment.
See *The Wild Hunt – The Hound Who Hunts Nightmares, Book One.*

2. *"I was at Mons ...".*
Dr Robinson is probably referring to *"The Angel of Mons"*, a legend that tells of a group of *warrior angels* (though some claimed they were not angels at all but rather the spirits of medieval archers, while others described their saviours as *"ghostly horsemen"*) who supposedly protected British troops during the Battle of Mons (Belgium, 23rd August 1914).

3. *The Unseen League*
A secret government organisation dedicated to protecting Britain from malign supernatural forces. *The League* was created by Sir Francis Walsingham in the late 1580s. At the time of its inception it was known, rather bizarrely, as *The Gentlemen Good Friends*, changing its name to *The Unseen League* some time in the 1700s. After World War Two, *The League* was modernised and renamed as *MI Unseen.*
See *Grendel – The Hound Who Hunts Nightmares, Book Two.*

4. Dylan and Don's Fishmongers
This would appear to be the code-name that *The Unseen League* was known by when it had to be reached via Directory Enquiries. The reference is obscure, but it might allude to the mythical *Dylan ail Don*, a character from the *Mabingion* (*a collection of stories from Welsh mythology*). His name translates as *"Dylan the Second Wave"*, meaning that he was the second born. This, in turn, might allude to *The Unseen League* being the second incarnation of Walsingham's original organisation (see note 2).

5. *"The Spaniard That Blighted My Life"*
A popular comic song of the early Twentieth Century. Composed (and performed) by the British Music Hall star Billy Merson in 1911, it was later made famous by Al Jolson.

6. Naik
In this instance, a corporal in the British Indian Army.

7. Garhwal Rifles
An infantry regiment in the British Indian Army. The Garhwal Rifles served with great distinction on the Western Front during the First World War.

8. Defence of Festubert
The Defence of Festubert (23-24 November, 1914) saw British and Indian troops defend the French village of Festubert against a German advance, and was one of the first examples of organised trench warfare.

9. Sepoy
An Indian soldier serving in the British Army.

10. Johnny Summers
An English boxer from Middlesbrough. Summers was the British Empire Welterweight Champion between 1912 and 1914. He made three defences of his title.

11. Gravenstafel Ridge
The Battle of Gravenstafel Ridge (22-23 April, 1915) was the first engagement of The Second Battle of Ypres (22 April – 25 May).

12. Battle of the Tardenois
The Battle of Tardenois (22-26 July, 1918). Allied troops (including the 51st Highlanders and the 62nd (2nd West Riding) Division forced the retreat of the German army through the Ardre Valley, France.

13. Pook Alberich Albi
The 19th Pook (King) of the Pharisees – the Elf tribe of southeast England.
See *The Wild Hunt – The Hound Who Hunts Nightmares, Book One*.

14. The Fancy
The Fancy were a collection of aristocrats, sportsmen and enthusiasts who organized and promoted the sport of boxing in the 18th and 19th centuries.

15. Camulos
A Celtic war god who the Romans equated with Mars. He was popular among many of the tribes of Gaul and Britain, especially the Belgic tribes. The Romano-British town (and former tribal capital of the Trinovantes and later the Catuvellauni) of Camulodunum, "Stronghold of Camulos" (now Colchester), was named in his honour, as well as, perhaps, the mythical stronghold of Camelot. His symbol was the wild boar.

16. The Remi
A Belgic tribe inhabiting northeastern Gaul.

17. The Nervii
A Gallic tribe that Julius Caesar considered the most warlike of the Belgic tribes.

18. Artauis
A Gallic god who the Romans equated with Mercury. In Gaulish his name means "bear".

19. *The Old Smoke*
London.

20. Whelk-faced Willie The Wheeze Willikins
The Goblin landlord of *The Concealed Arms*, and co-founder (with Cornelius Lyons) of *The Bridge Club*.
See *The King Of Avalon – The Hound Who Hunts Nightmares, Book Three*.

Here, Willie is misquoting Samuel Johnson's famous remark that – *"When a man is tired of London he is tired of life; for there is in London all that life can afford."*

21. The Mound
A secret prison run by The Unseen League for criminals and political prisoners of a supernatural persuasion.
See *Grendel – The Hound Who Hunts Nightmares, Book Two*.

22. Rudiobus
A (rather obscure) Celtic horse god.

23. Carnutes
A powerful Celtic tribe of central Gaul.

24. The Achilles Project
A series of projects created by *The Unseen League/MI Unseen* that attempted (some with success, some not!) to use the powers of the supernatural for the benefit and defence of the realm. To date there are twelve known Achilles Projects, though the rumoured *Achilles Project XIII* has become the centre of much speculation and concern.
Two projects have so far been discussed in the papers of *Lyons & Hound* (est 1895):

Achilles Project VI – The Shadow Soldiers. An attempt to give selected *MI Unseen Agents* enhanced powers by injecting them with a serum derived from the blood of vampires.
By all accounts the enterprise ended in a bloody catastrophe.

Achilles Project IX – which saw the creation of *MI Unseen* spies of mixed human and Elf heritage.

The projects take their name from Britain's first officially recognised *super-soldier*, the legendary Sergeant Bob 'Slasher' Harrington (*The Achilles of Waterloo*).

The works of
Caractacus Plume

The Hound Who Hunts Nightmares

The Case Of The Lost Crowns Of Albion

The Wild Hunt
Grendel
The King Of Avalon

From The Casebook Of Lyons & Hound

Incident At Five Hundred Acre Wood

www.caractacusplume.com

Silvatici Publishing
silvatici@outlook.com

Made in the USA
Columbia, SC
10 February 2018